The lady's temper is trying his nerves.

Amelia turned scarlet and for a moment Logan wondered if she might give him a good whack with the parasol she was twisting in her hands. She did nothing, said nothing, but returned his stare with such umbrage that Logan was very nearly taken aback.

"Good day, Mr. Reed. I no longer wish to listen to anything you have to say," Amelia said and turned to leave, but Logan reached out to halt her.

She fixed him with a stony stare that would have crumbled a less stalwart foe. "Unhand me, sir!"

"You sure run hot and cold, lady." Logan's voice was husky and his eyes were narrowed ever so slightly. "But either way, one thing you'd better learn quickly—and I'm not saying this to put you off again," he said pausing to tighten his grip in open defiance of her demand, "listening to me may very well save your life."

"When you say something that seems life-saving," she murmured, "I will listen with the utmost regard." She pulled her arm away and gathered her skirts in hand. "Good day, Mr. Reed."

Tracie J. Peterson is one of **Heartsong Presents'** most popular authors. She makes her home in Kansas with her husband and three children. Tracie has also written eight successful **Heartsong Presents** titles under the name of Janelle Jamison.

HEARTSONG PRESENTS

Don't miss out on any of our super romances. Write to us at the following address for information on available titles, newest releases, and club information.

Heartsong Presents Readers' Service
P.O. Box 719
Uhrichsville, OH 44683

Logan's Lady

Tracie J. Peterson

Heartsong Presents

Dedicated to: Rebecca Germany,
one of my favorite editors.
Your friendship means a great deal to me and I
thank God upon my every remembrance of you.

A note from the Author:
I love to hear from my readers! You may correspond
with me by writing:

Tracie J. Peterson
Author Relations
P.O. Box 719
Uhrichsville, OH 44683

ISBN 1-57748-154-2

LOGAN'S LADY

Cover illustration by Victoria Lisi and Julius.

PRINTED IN THE U.S.A.

one

Colorado, 1875

Amelia grimaced as she heard her father and Sir Jeffery Chamberlain break into yet another discussion on the implementation of fertilizer to boost agricultural yields. *It was this dreadful country that did it,* she thought. *America! A country filled with barbaric men, ill-mannered women and positively rotten children.*

Shifting uncomfortably in the seat of their stage, Amelia wished fervently that if there were a God, He would reach down and smite the lot of them in order that she might be allowed to return home to England. But of course that wasn't going to happen because Amelia had firmly decided for herself that there was no God.

"I say, Chamberlain," her father stated with a marginal note of enthusiasm. "I believe we're slowing down."

"Yes, quite right," the younger man responded and peered out the window. "We've made an excellent way thanks to our time spent on the railroad. American railroads are quite the thing. Good money here, what?"

"Indeed, the stage coaches are just as abominable as those back home, but I believe their railway system to be quite superior," came the reply and the conversation erupted into a spirited discussion of the American rail system. Amelia sighed, adjusted her lace collar and waited for the announcement that they had arrived in some small, forsaken Colorado town.

She hadn't wanted to come on this trip to America. America had been the furthest thing from her mind, in fact, but her father was insistent and clearly closed the matter to discussion. Amelia's sisters Penelope and Margaret were just as loath to travel, but they were quite interested in Sir Jeffery Chamberlain.

Amelia held a small wish that she could share their enthusiasm. After all, he was to become her husband. At least that was the plan as her father saw it, but Amelia had no intention of marrying the pompous man. Jeffery Chamberlain was a long time crony of her father's. He wasted his days doing as little as possible, furthering his already sound reputation of being a spoiled dandy. He had been knighted, but only because his mother held a tender place in the queen's heart. And, he owned vast estates with wondrous woods that beckoned the visitor to take a turn about, but those were his only redeeming qualities as far as Amelia was concerned.

Her father viewed him in a different light, however. Sir Jeffery Chamberlain was rich and popular with Queen Victoria's court. He had a sound education and a quick wit which had managed to keep him out of trouble on more than one occasion, and he was worth an enormous sum of money which could keep not only his own lands well-kept, but would surely flow over to his future father-in-law, Lord Reginald Amhurst, the sixth earl of Donneswick—should that need arise.

Staring hard at the man, Amelia noted all of his flaws. His nose was too long, his forehead too shiny. He had perfect white teeth which seemed to be constantly bared for all the world behind unflattering smiles and his beady eyes were placed too close together. Added to this, the man was an unmitigated bore.

Amelia shook her head uncomfortably and tried against the rocking and bouncing of the stage to look at the magazine she'd bought in Cheyenne. Flipping through pages of ladies' fashions, Amelia tried to rationalize her thoughts. *I cannot blame Father for setting out to arrange a marriage. It is done all the time in my circle of friends. Why, I don't even remember the last time one of my companions managed to marry for love, and not because the union was of financial benefit to one family or the other.* Some of her friends had grown to genuinely love their intended mates. Others had not. Her dear friend and confidant, Sarah Greene, had managed to find herself engaged to a charming man of wit and gentlemanly breeding and had quickly lost her heart. But that was not to be the case for Amelia. She could not find it in her heart to love Sir Jeffery, as he insisted they call him, nor did she think love would grow there for this man.

Amidst a roar of "whoa's" and a cloud of dust, Amelia realized that they had come to a stop. Ignoring her father's window description of the town, Amelia tucked the magazine into her bag. Immediately Penelope and Margaret began fussing and going on about the wilds of America.

"I suppose we might very well be scalped by Indians," Penelope said with a fearful expression. She allowed Sir Jeffery to assist her from the stage before adding, "We're so very glad to have your company, Sir Jeffery." She oozed congeniality and interlaced her arm with his. At seventeen she was more than a little bit aware of the power a young women's simpering could have over the male gender.

"It is my pleasure, Miss Penelope," he assured her.

Margaret, a year Penelope's junior, secured her place on the opposite arm of Sir Jeffery as soon as her father had helped her from the stage. "Yes, it would be quite frightful to have come all this way into the heart of the American wilderness with only Father and Mattersley to offer protection. Why, whatever would three women and two old men do should the heathens truly choose to attack us?" Mattersley, the other *old man* she referred to was the earl's manservant and constant companion.

Amelia watched all this through the open door of the stage. She rolled her eyes and sighed. *Indeed, what would Sir Jeffery, pompous dandy that he was, do in such a situation? Bore the poor Indians to death with questions of what fertilizer they were using on the Colorado plains?* She couldn't abide the simpering of her sisters and chose instead to remain in her seat on the stage until her father beckoned her forward.

"Amelia, allow me to help you down. Why, you've scarcely said two words since we left Cheyenne. You aren't ill are you? Taken with vapors, what?"

Amelia's pale blue eyes met those of her father's. "No, Father, I'm not at all indisposed. I simply have had my mind consumed with a variety of subjects."

Sir Jeffery untangled himself from Amelia's sisters and came to offer his hand. "May I accompany you to the hotel, Lady Amhurst?" he questioned with a slight bow. Amelia noticed her father's frown as if he could read the curt reply she was thinking. Containing her thoughts with absolute ladylike control, she nodded. "Of course. Thank you," she murmured, putting her gloved fingers into Jeffery's palm.

"I have arranged for us to have rooms at a boarding house here in Greeley," the earl began. "It's a temperance colony so there will be no wine with dinner, nor any after-dinner brandy, I'm afraid." Amelia, knowing her father's distaste for alcohol, realized that he said the latter for Jeffery's sake.

"Ah, the barbarians," Jeffery sighed and Amelia knew he meant it. To Jeffery, any measure of discomfort represented a less than acceptable social standing. And for Jeffery to be without his brandy was definitely a discomfort.

For a reason beyond her understanding, Amelia was put out at Jeffery's attitude. Not because of the alcohol—although she herself couldn't abide the stuff—no, it was more than simple issues of food and drink. Jeffery's entire demeanor put her at odds. Maybe it was just that she wanted to conflict with his ideals. Maybe it was the fact that she was completely disgusted with his companionship and still hadn't been able to get it across to either her father or Jeffery that she had no desire to marry.

Glancing upward, Amelia instantly felt the noon sun bear down on her. Grimacing, she opened her white parasol and lifted it overhead to ward off the harsh rays.

"Oh, Father," Penelope began to whine, "it's ever so hot here. Must we stand about as though we were hired help?" She looked for all the world as though she might faint dead away at any moment.

They were all quite used to Penelope and Margaret's displays of weakness, and for several moments no one said anything. Finally the earl motioned for his loyal valet, Mattersley, and gave him several coins. "See if you can't arrange for our things to be brought up." The man, close in age to his employer, gave a regal bow and set out on his mission. "There," the earl said, turning to the party, "I'd say that settled itself rather nicely. Let's make our way up, what?"

"Indeed," Jeffery answered as though his was the only opinion to be had. "This harsh American sun is quite hard on fair English skin." He said the words looking at Amelia, but she had the distinct impression they were given more in consideration of his own situation than of hers.

The dry, dusty streets of Greeley did nothing to encourage the entourage. The boarding house was a far cry from the regal estate they'd left behind in England. It wasn't even as nice as the furnishings they'd acquired in New York City or Chicago. In fact, Amelia knew it was by far the worst accommodations they'd known yet, and her opinion of America slipped even lower. Why, even when they'd toured India, they'd resided on lovely estates.

From the moment they walked into the questionable place, arguments ensued and miseries were heightened. The owners of the atrocious little house actually expected Amelia and her sisters to share one bed. The very thought of it caused Penelope to cry and Margaret to fan herself feverishly as though she might actually faint from the very suggestion.

"I believe we'd arranged to have all five of your rooms," the earl protested, combating a roving horde of black flies.

"Kain't hep it a bit, mister," the slovenly dressed proprietor announced. "I hed a man come in last night what needed a place to stay."

"This is Reginald Amhurst, the sixth earl of Donneswick," Chamberlain interjected angrily. "Lord Amhurst, to you."

The proprietor looked over the rim of his dirty spectacles. "Ferenors, eh? We gets 'em all kinds here. You sound to be them thar British gents. I guess the missus said you was comin'."

Amelia grew tired with the exchange and glanced around the room to where a crude painting hung at the base of the stairs. She studied it intently, wishing she could forget the heat. The picture fascinated her from afar, as it seemed to almost move with life. Stepping closer, Amelia found it half covered with pesky black flies. It was only then that she really noticed most everything suffered from such a fate.

"Excuse me," a stranger's voice sounded over her head. "This isn't an art gallery. Besides, I don't think old Farley's painting is all that interesting."

Amelia was so lost in thought that she hadn't realized she was blocking the stairway. She looked up with a surprised expression and found herself noticing the broad, muscular frame that accompanied the voice. The mustached mouth seemed to twitch a bit as though it might break into a laugh.

Without so much as a smile, Amelia backed away. "My pardon, Sir." Her voice was haughty and her look froze the man in his place. She still found it disconcerting to be openly addressed by men without a proper introduction. Childhood teachings were hard to lay aside, even for a holiday to America.

With a grin, he gave a broad sweep. "You are quite pardoned, Ma'am."

Amelia raised her handkerchief and turned away to keep from muttering something most unladylike. *Rude. That's what all Americans are.*

"Hey thar, Logan," the boarding house proprietor called as the man passed to the front door.

"Afternoon, Ted."

Amelia tried to watch the scene without letting the man called Logan see she was at all interested in the conversation.

"Logan, didn't ya tell me you was gonna be leadin' a group of ferenors up the mountains?"

"I did."

"Well, I think this here party be yer folks."

Logan eyed the group suspiciously as though he'd just been told that they were responsible for having robbed the local bank.

"You're Earl Donneswick?" Logan questioned Amelia's father.

"I am, indeed." Lord Amhurst replied, before Jeffery could speak. Amelia turned to watch the introduction. "This is Sir Jeffery Chamberlain, my man Mattersley, and my daughters."

Logan let his gaze travel around the room to each of the women before settling on Amelia. He smiled slightly when his blatant stare caused her to blush, then turned his attention to the matter at hand.

"I'm Logan Reed, your guide to Estes Park."

"Mr. Reed, we are quite anxious to be started on our journey. Can you advise us as to when we might expect to begin? The heat is positively wilting our ladies." Jeffery commented before the earl could do the same.

Logan looked again at the women. "Are you proposing to take your womenfolk along?"

"Indeed we are," the earl replied.

Amelia watched as Logan cast a skeptical glance at her. "There are places where we'll scarcely have a trail to follow. Packing into the Rockies isn't a Sunday school picnic."

"My daughters have climbed in the Alps, my good man. I assure you they are quite up to the challenge."

Logan's smile broadened. "If you say so. I just wouldn't want the ladies to get hurt." His gaze returned to Amelia who stuck her chin in the air defiantly and turned toward the fly-covered window.

"Lady Amhurst and her sisters are quite capable," Jeffery interjected irritably.

"Lady Amhurst? I thought you said your name was Donneswick."

The earl smiled tolerantly. "I am Reginald Amhurst, the sixth earl of Donneswick. I am called Lord Amhurst, but it is common when I travel abroad to have my title mistaken for my name. My daughters, of course, are called by the family name of Amhurst. A bit confusing for you Yanks, but nevertheless, easy enough to remember."

"With that matter resolved," Chamberlain stated in a cool, even voice, "when can we expect to begin? You surely can't expect us to remain in this poor excuse for a town for much longer."

"Whoa, now. Just hold on for a minute," Logan said raising his hand. Amelia glanced back over her shoulder, fascinated in spite of herself at the way Logan Reed seemed to naturally take charge. "We've got some ground rules to cover first and I don't think standing around the front door of Ted's is the place for it. Ted, can we use the dining room?"

"Sure enuf, Logan. Ya go right ahead." Ted seemed to be happy to rid himself of the commotion. "Ya want I should have the missus bring somethin' to drink?"

He addressed Logan, but it was Lord Amhurst who answered. "Yes, please have tea and cakes sent 'round."

Ted stared at the man for a moment, then turned to Logan. "It's okay, Ted. Why don't you just bring whatever's at hand." This the man understood and nodded agreement before taking himself off to the kitchen.

The party stared collectively at Logan, barely tolerating his breach of etiquette, but Amelia was certain that for Mr. Logan Reed, breaching etiquette was probably a daily routine.

"Come on this way," Logan ordered and led the way without even waiting to hear an approval from the earl or Jeffery. The entourage followed, murmuring among themselves as to the character and manners of the tall man.

"Everybody might as well sit down," Logan said, giving his well-worn hat a toss to the sideboard.

Amelia watched in complete amazement. At home, in England, her father would never have been addressed in such a manner. At home he commanded respect and held a position of complete authority. Here in America, however, he was just a man and it didn't matter in the least that he was titled.

While Amelia stood in motionless study, Logan pulled out a chair and offered it to her. Her blue eyes met the rich warmth of his green ones. She studied his face for a moment longer, noting the trimmed mustache and square, but newly shaven jaw.

"Thank you," she murmured and slipped into her chair without taking her gaze from his face.

"Now, we need to discuss this matter in some detail," Logan announced. He stood at the head of the table looking as though he were some famed orator about to impart great knowledge upon the masses.

"Mr. Reed," Amelia's father interrupted. "I have an understanding with the owner of several cabins in the Estes Park valley. He assured me that he would send a guide to bring our party to Estes. Furthermore, there is to be another family accompanying us; Lord and Lady Gambett and their two daughters."

Logan nodded. "I know about the Gambetts and was headed up to speak to them when you arrived. According to Ted, they're staying on the other end of town at Widow Compton's place. I suppose they're planning to bring their womenfolk along as well?"

"Indeed, they are. What, may I ask, is the difficulty here?"

Logan ran a hand through his brown hair and sighed. "The problem is this: I wasn't expecting to have to pack women into the mountains. No one mentioned women at all, in fact. I was told I'd be taking a hunting party to Estes. A hunting party seemed to lend itself to the idea of men."

Amelia suppressed a laugh and received the stunned glances of her traveling companions.

"You have something to say here, Miss. . ." Logan paused as if trying to remember which name she was to be addressed by.

"I am Lady Amhurst. Lady Amelia Amhurst. And while we're to discuss this trip, then yes, I suppose I do have a few things to say." She ignored the frown on her father's face and the "darling, please be silent" glare of Jeffery. "In England, women quite often ride to the hunt. We enjoy sporting as much as our menfolk. Furthermore, I assure you, we are quite capable of handling a gun, a mount, and any other hardship that might present itself on the trip."

"I'm glad to hear that you are so capable, Lady Amhurst. You won't be offended then when I state my rules. We will begin at sunrise. That doesn't mean we'll get up at sunrise, have a leisurely tea, and be on the road by nine. It means things packed, on your horse, ready to ride at sunrise. We'll head into Longmont first, which will give you a last chance at a night's rest in bed before a week of sleeping on the ground. If you're short on supplies you can pick them up there."

No one said a word and even Amelia decided against protesting, at least until she'd heard the full speech.

Logan continued. "It gets cold at night. We'll eventually be 7,000 feet up and the air will be thinner. Every morning you'll find hoarfrost on the ground so staying dry and warm will be your biggest priority. Each of you will pack at least three blankets and a canteen. Again, if you don't have them, pick them up here in Greeley or get them in Longmont. If you don't have them, you don't go. Also, there will be no sidesaddles available. You women will be required to ride astride, so dress accordingly. Oh, and everyone wears a good, sturdy pair of boots. This is important both for riding and for walking if your horse should go lame."

"Mr. Reed!" Lord Amhurst began to protest. "You cannot expect my daughters to ride astride these American horses. First of all it is most unacceptable and second, it—"

"If they don't ride astride, they don't go," Logan replied flatly. "Having them riding sidesaddle is more danger than I'm willing to take on. If you want them to come out of this alive, they need to have every possible chance at staying that way."

"Perhaps, Amhurst," Jeffery addressed him less formally, "we could arrange to employ another guide."

Logan laughed and crossed his arms against his chest. "I challenge you to find one. I'm one of only two in the area who will even bother with you people."

"And what, pray tell, is that supposed to mean?" Amelia interjected.

Logan met her eyes. "It means, I resent European tourists and rich socialites who come to take the air in my mountains. They don't care for the real beauty at hand and they never stay longer than it takes to abuse what they will before going off to boast of their conquests. I made a promise, however, to pack you folks into Estes, but you," he pointed a finger at each of the women, "are completely unsuited for the challenge. There are far too many things to consider when it comes to women. Your physical constitution is weaker, not to mention that by nature being a woman lends itself to certain other types of physical complications and private needs."

"See here! You have no right to talk that way in front of these ladies," Chamberlain protested.

"That is exactly the kind of coddling I'm talking about. It has no place on a mountain ridge. I am not trying to make this unpleasant, but we must establish some rules here in order to keep you folks from dying on the way." Logan's voice lowered to a near whisper. "I won't have their blood on my hands, just because they are too proud and arrogant to take direction from someone who's had more experience." He said "they", but his steely gaze was firmly fixed on Amelia.

"What other rules would you have us abide by, Mr. Reed?" the earl finally asked.

"No alcohol of any kind. No shooting animals on the way to Estes. No stopping for tea four times a day and no special treatment of anyone in the party. If you can't cut it, you go back." Logan took a deep breath. "Finally, my word is law. I know this land and what it's capable of. When I tell you that something needs to be done a certain way, I expect it to be done without question. Even if it pertains to something that shocks your genteel constitutions. I'm not a hard man to get along with," he said pausing again, "but I find the institutions of nobility a bit trying. If I should call you by something other than by your privileged titles, I'll expect you to over-look it. During a rock slide it could be difficult to remember if I'm to address you by earl, lady, or your majesty. My main objective is to get your party to Estes in as close to one piece as possible. That's all."

"I suppose we can live with these rules of yours," Lord Amhurst replied. "Ladies, can you manage?" Penelope and Margaret looked to Amelia and back to their father before nodding their heads.

"Well, Amelia?" her father questioned and all eyes turned to her.

Facing Logan with a confident glare, she replied, "I can certainly meet any challenge that Mr. Reed is capable of delivering."

Logan laughed. "Well, I'm capable of delivering quite a bit, believe me."

two

Amelia spent the remainder of the afternoon listening to her sisters alternate between their praises of Sir Jeffery and their concerns about the trip.

"You are such a bore, Amelia," Penelope said with little concern for the harshness of her tone. "Why, Jeffery has simply devoted himself to you on this trip and you've done nothing but act as though you could not care less."

"I *couldn't* care less," Amelia assured her sister.

"But the man is to be your husband. Father arranged this entire trip just to bring you two closer. I think it was rather sporting of Jeffery to endure the open way you stared at that Reed fellow."

Amelia gasped. "I did not stare at Mr. Reed!"

"You did," Margaret confirmed. "I saw you."

Amelia shook her head. "I can't be bothered with you two twittering ninnies. Besides, I never said I approved of Father's arrangement for Sir Jeffery to become my husband. I have no intentions of getting closer to the man and certainly none of marrying him."

"I think Sir Jeffery is wonderful. You're just being mean and spiteful," Penelope stated with a stamp of her foot. A little cloud of dust rose from the floor along with several flies.

"If you think he's so wonderful Penelope, why don't you marry him?" Amelia snapped. The heat was making her grumpy and her sister's interrogation was making her angry.

"I'd love to marry him," Margaret said in a daft and dreamy way that Amelia thought epitomized the typical addle-brained girl.

"I shall speak to Father about it immediately," Amelia said sarcastically. "Perhaps he will see the sense in it." *If only he would.*

Margaret stared after her with open mouth, while Penelope took the whole thing with an air of indifference. "You know it doesn't matter what you want, Amelia. Father must marry you off before you turn twenty-one this autumn, or lose mother's money. Her fortune means a great deal to him. Surely you wouldn't begrudge your own father his mainstay."

Amelia looked at her younger sisters for a moment. As fair-haired as she, yet more finely featured and petite, Amelia had no doubt that they saw her as some sort of ogre who thought only of herself. Their mother's fortune, a trust set in place by their grandmother, was specifically held for the purpose that none of her daughters need feel pressured to marry for money. The money would, in fact, pass to each daughter on her twenty-first birthday, if she were still unmarried. If the girls married before that time, the money reverted to the family coffers and could be used by their father, for the benefit of all as he saw fit. Amelia knew it was this which drove her father forward to see her married to Sir Jeffery.

"I have no desire for Father to concern himself with his financial well-being. However, there are things that matter deeply to me, and Jeffery Chamberlain is not one of them." With that Amelia left the room, taking up her parasol. By the time she'd reached the bottom step she'd decided that a walk to consider the rest of Greeley was in order.

Parasol high, Amelia passed from the house in a soft, almost silent swishing of her pale pink afternoon dress. She was nearly to the corner of the boarding house when she caught the sound of voices and immediately recognized one of them to be Logan Reed's.

"You sure asked for it this time, Logan. Hauling those

prissy misses all the way over the mountain to Estes ain't gonna be an easy ride," an unidentified man was stating.

"No, it won't," Logan said, sounding very disturbed. "Women are always trouble. I guess next time Evans sends me over, I'll be sure and ask who all is supposed to come back with me."

"It might save you some grief at that. Still," the man said with a pause, "they sure are purty girls. They look as fine as old Bart's spittoon after a Sunday shining."

Amelia paled at the comparison, while Logan laughed. How she wished she could face him and tell him just what she thought of Americans and their spittoons. It seemed every man in this wretched country had taken up that particularly nasty habit of chewing and spitting. *No doubt Mr. Reed will be no exception.*

"I don't think I'd compliment any of them in exactly those words, Ross. These are refined British women." Amelia straightened her shoulders a bit and thought perhaps she'd misjudged Logan Reed. Logan's next few words, however, completely destroyed any further doubt. "They are the most uppity creatures God ever put on the face of the earth. They have a queen for a monarch and it makes them feel mighty important."

Amelia seethed. *How dare he even mention the queen. He isn't fit to. . .* The thought faded as Logan continued.

"The Brits are the hardest of all to work with. The Swedes come and they're just a big bunch of land-loving, life-loving primitives. The Germans are much the same and always bring a lot of life to a party. But the Brits think everything goes from their mouth to God's ear. They are rude and insensitive to other people and expect to stop on a ledge two feet wide, or any other dangerous or unseemly place, if it dares to be time for tea. In fact, I'd wager good money that before I even get this party packed halfway through the foothills, one of those 'purty' women, as you call them, will expect to have tea and biscuits on a silver tray."

At this, Amelia could take no more. She whipped around the corner in a fury. Angered beyond reason and filled with rage, she took her stand. "How dare you insult my family and friends in such a manner. I have never been so enraged in all of my twenty years!" She barely paused to take a breath. "I have traveled all across Europe and India and never in my life have I met more rude and insensitive people than here in America. If you want to see difficulty and stubbornness, Mr. Reed, I'm certain you have no further to go than the mirror in your room." At this she stormed off, feeling quite vindicated.

છ

Logan stared after her with a mocking grin on his lips. He'd known full-well she was eavesdropping and intended to take her to task for it quite solidly. The man beside him, uncomfortable with the display of temper, quickly excused himself and ran with long strides toward the busier part of town. When Logan began to chuckle out loud, Amelia turned back indignantly.

"Whatever are you snickering about?" Amelia questioned, her cheeks flushed from the sun and the encounter. Apparently remembering her parasol, she raised it to shield her skin.

"I'm amused," Logan said in a snooty tone, mocking her.

"I see nothing at all funny here. You have insulted good people, Mr. Reed. Gentlefolk, from the lineage of nobility, with more grace and manners than you could ever hope to attain. People, I might add, who are paying you a handsome wage to do a job."

She was breathing heavily. Beads of perspiration were forming on her brow. Her blue eyes were framed by long blond lashes that curled away from her eyes like rays of sunshine through a storm cloud. She reminded Logan of a china doll with her bulk of blond hair piled high on her head, complete with fashionable hat. Logan thought he'd never seen a more beautiful woman, but he still desired to put her into her place once and for all.

"And does your family consider eavesdropping to be one of those gracious manners of which you speak so highly?" he questioned, taking long easy strides to where she stood. Amelia recoiled as though she had been slapped.

"I see you find my words disconcerting," Logan said, his face now serious. Amelia, speechless, only returned his blatant stare. "People with manners, Miss," he paused, then shook his head. "No, make that Lady Amhurst. Anyway, people of true refinement have no need to advertise it or crow it from the rooftops. They show it in action. And they need not make others feel less important by using flashy titles and snobbery. I don't believe eavesdropping would be considered a substantial way to prove one's merit in any society."

Amelia found her tongue at last. "I never intended to eavesdrop, Mr. Reed," she said emphasizing the title. "I was simply taking in a bit of air, a very little bit I might add. Is it my fault that your voice carries above the sounds of normal activity?"

Logan laughed. "I could excuse a simple wandering-in, but you stood there a full five minutes before making your presence known. I said what I said, knowing full well you were there. I wanted to see just how much you would take before jumping me."

Amelia's expression tightened. "You couldn't possibly have known I was there. I had just come from the front of the house and I was making no noise."

Logan's amusement was obviously stated in his eyes. He stepped back to the house, pulling Amelia with him. Leaving Amelia to stand in stunned silence at his bold touch, he went around the corner. "What do you see, Lady Amhurst?"

Amelia looked to the corner of the house. "I see nothing. Whatever are you talking about?"

"Look again. You're going to have to have a sharper sense of the obvious if you're to survive in the wilds of Colorado."

From around the corner Logan waited a long moment before deciding he wasn't being quite fair. He reached up and adjusted his hat hoping his shadow's movement on the ground would catch her eye.

"Very well, Mr. Reed," Amelia sounded humbled. "I see your point, but it could have just as easily been one of my sisters. You couldn't possibly have known it was me and not one of them."

Logan looked around the corner with a self-satisfied expression on his face. "You're a little more robust, shall we say, than your sisters." His gaze trailed the length of her body before coming again to rest on her face.

Amelia turned scarlet and for a moment Logan wondered if she might give him a good whack with the parasol she was twisting in her hands. She did nothing, said nothing, but returned his stare with such umbrage that Logan was very nearly taken aback.

"Good day, Mr. Reed. I no longer wish to listen to anything you have to say," Amelia said and turned to leave, but Logan reached out to halt her.

She fixed him with a stony stare that would have crumbled a less stalwart foe.

"Unhand me, sir!"

"You sure run hot and cold, lady." Logan's voice was husky and his eyes were narrowed ever so slightly. "But either way, one thing you'd better learn quickly—and I'm not saying this to put you off again," he said pausing to tighten his grip in open defiance of her demand, "listening to me may very well save your life."

"When you say something that seems life-saving," she murmured, "I will listen with the utmost regard." She pulled her arm away and gathered her skirts in hand. "Good day, Mr. Reed."

Logan watched her walk away in her facade of fire and ice. She was unlike any woman he'd ever met in his life—and he'd certainly met many a fine lady in his day. She was strong and self-assured and Logan knew that if the entire party perished in the face of their mountain challenge, Amelia would survive and probably thrive.

He liked her, he decided. He liked her a great deal. For all her snooty ways and uppity suggestions, she was growing more interesting by the minute and Logan intended to take advantage of the long summer months to come in which he'd be a part of her Estes Park stay.

Logan stood in a kind of stupor for a few more minutes, until the voice of Lord Amhurst sounded from behind him.

"Mr. Reed," he began, "I should like to inquire as to our accommodations. The proprietor here tells me that you have taken one of the rooms intended for our use. I would like to have it back."

"Sorry," Logan said without feeling the least bit apologetic. "I'm gonna need a good night's rest if I'm to lead you all to Longmont. It isn't anything personal and I'm sorry Ted parceled out your evening comforts, but I need the room."

The earl looked taken back for a moment, apparently unaccustomed to his requests being refused, but nodded as he acquiesced to the circumstances.

Logan took off before the man could say another word. He could have given up the room easily, but his pride made him rigid. "Oh Lord," he whispered, "I should have been kinder. When I settle down a bit, I'll go back to the earl of Donneswick and give him the room." Logan rounded the corner of the house and found Penelope, Margaret, and Chamberlain sitting beneath the community shade tree. It was the only shade tree on this side of town. He couldn't help but wonder where Amelia had gone, then chided himself for even thinking of her. There'd be time enough on the trip, not to mention when they reached Estes, to learn more about her. He could take his time, he reasoned, remembering that Evans had told him the party would stay until first snow.

Whistling a tune, Logan made his way past Amelia's simpering sisters, tipped his hat ever so slightly, and headed for the livery. Lady Amelia Amhurst, he thought with a sudden revelation. "There's no reason she can't be my lady," Logan stated aloud to no one in particular. "No reason at all."

three

The following day brought the hunting party together. Lord and Lady Gambett arrived with their whiny daughters Henrietta and Josephine. Both of the girls were long-time companions of Penelope and Margaret, and their reunion was one of excited giggles and squeals of delight. Amelia stood beneath the shade of the community tree and waited for the party to move out to Longmont. She studied the landscape around her and decided she was very glad not to live in this dusty community of flies and harsh prairie winds. To the west she noted the Rocky Mountains and though they were beautiful, she would have happily passed up the chance to further explore them—if her father would have given her the option to return home.

Lady Gambett fussed over her daughters like a mother hen, voicing her concern quite loudly that they should have to wear such a monstrous apparatus as what the store clerk had called a "lady's mountain dress." The outfit appeared for all intents and purposes to be no different from any other riding habit. A long serviceable skirt of blue serge fell to the boot tops of each young lady, while underneath, a fuller, billowing version of a petticoat allowed the freedom to ride astride.

Amelia knew her own attire to be quite comfortable and didn't really mind the idea of trading in her dainty sidesaddle for the fuller and more masculine McClellan cavalry saddle. She'd heard Lady Bird speak of these at one of her lectures on the Rockies and just remembering the older woman made Amelia smile. Lady Isabella Bird was a remarkable woman.

Traveling all over the world to the wildest reaches was nothing to this adventuresome lady. She had come to the Rockies only two years earlier on her way back from the Sandwich Islands. By sheer grit and force of will, Lady Bird had placed herself in the hands of strangers and eventually into the hands of no one at all when she took a rugged Indian pony and traveled throughout the Rocky Mountains all alone. Amelia admired that kind of gumption. She'd never dreamed of doing something so incredible herself, but she thought Lady Bird's accounts of the solitude sounded refreshing. Watching the stars fade into the dawn Amelia wondered to herself what it might be like to lay out on a mountain top, under the stars and trees, with no other human being around for miles and miles.

"You look pretty tolerable when you smile like that," Logan's voice sounded in her ear.

Startled, Amelia instantly drew back and lost the joy of her self-reflection. "Haven't you better things to do, Mr. Reed? As I recall, we were to be on our way by now. What seems to be keeping us?"

Logan smiled. "Loose shoe on one of the horses. Should have it fixed in a quick minute."

Amelia hoped this would end their conversation, but it didn't.

"You gonna be able to ride in that?" Logan asked seriously, pointing to the wind-blown navy blue skirt which blew just high enough to reveal matching bloomers beneath.

Amelia felt her face grow hot. "I assure you I will be quite able to ride. This outfit is especially designed to allow a woman to ride astride. Just as you demanded."

"Good. I don't want any of you dainty ladies to be pitched over the side."

Amelia jutted her chin out defiantly and said nothing. Logan Reed was clearly the most incorrigible man she'd ever met in her life and she wasn't about to let him get the best of her.

"Logan!" A man hollered and waved from where the others were gathered. "Horse is ready."

"Well, Lady Amhurst, I believe we are about to get underway," Logan said with a low sweeping bow.

❧

Amelia was hot and dirty and very unhappy when the party at last rode into Longmont, Colorado. The day had not been a pleasant one for Amelia. Her sisters had squabbled almost half the way about who was going to wear the blue-veiled straw riding bonnet. Penelope had latched on to it in Greeley, but Margaret had soon learned the benefits of her sister's veil and insisted she trade her. Margaret had protested that as the youngest, at sixteen, she was also the more delicate of the trio. Josephine, Margaret's bosom companion, heartily agreed. Pushing up tiny round spectacles, Josephine was only coming to realize the protection her glasses offered from the dust. While the others were delicately blotting their eyes with lace handkerchiefs, Josephine's eyes had remained a little more sheltered.

This argument over the bonnet, along with Logan's sneering grins and her father's constant manipulation to see her and Jeffery riding together, made Amelia want to run screaming in the direction of the nearest railroad station. But of course, convention denied her the possibility of such a display.

Glancing around at the small town of Longmont, Amelia was amused to see the townsfolk apparently could not even decide on the town's spelling. Some signs read *Longmount,* while others gave the title *Longmont.* The name St. Vrain seemed to be quite popular. There was the St. Vrain Cafe, the St. Vrain Saloon, and the St. Vrain Hotel which looked to her to be an oasis in the desert. Brilliantly white against the sun's light, the two story hotel beckoned the weary travelers forward and Amelia couldn't wait to sink into a hot bath.

Upon alighting from her horse, it was instantly apparent that Longmont suffered the same plague of black flies that had held Greeley under siege. The flies instantly clung to her riding habit and bonnet, leaving Amelia feeling as though her skin were crawling. The Gambett girls and her sisters were already whining about the intolerable conditions and although Amelia whole-heartedly agreed with their analysis that this town was completely forgotten by any kind of superior being, she refused to raise her voice in complaint.

"I assure you, ladies," Logan said with a hint of amusement in his tired voice, "this place is neither forsaken by God, nor condemned. The people here are friendly and helpful, if you treat them with respect. There's a well-stocked hardware store down Main Street, and if you ladies wish to purchase another veiled bonnet, you can try the mercantile just over there."

The words were meant to embarrass her sisters, but as far as Amelia could tell, neither Penelope nor Margaret were aware of Logan's intent.

"Remember, this is one of those trips where you'll have to do for yourself," Logan said, motioning to the pack mules. "You might just as well get used to that fact here and now. No one is going to care for you, or handle your things, but you. You'll be responsible for your bags and any personal items you choose to bring on this trip. Although, for the sake of your horses, the mules, and even yourselves, I suggest you greatly limit what you bring along."

Jeffery immediately appeared at Amelia's side. "Never fear, Lady Amhurst, I am your faithful servant. You find a comfortable place to rest and I will retrieve your things."

Amelia watched Logan's lips curl into a self-satisfied smile. Obviously he had pegged her for one of those who would choose to be waited on hand and foot. What further irritated her was that if Logan had not been there, she would have taken Chamberlain up on his offer.

"Never mind that," she said firmly. "I can manage, just as Mr. Reed has made clear I must." She pulled down her bedroll and bags without another glance at Logan.

"Surely there is no reason you cannot accept my help," Jeffery spoke from her side. He reached out to take hold of her bedroll. "I mean to say, you are a gentlewoman—a lady. It is hardly something Mr. Reed would understand, but certainly it does not escape my breeding to intercede on your behalf."

Amelia wearied of his nonsensical speech. She glared up at Jeffery harshly and pulled her bags away from his hands. "I am of sturdy stock, I assure you. I have climbed in the Alps without assistance from you." She couldn't help remembering the bevy of servants who had assisted her. "I have also barged the Nile, lived through an Indian monsoon, and endured the tedium of life at court. I surely can carry baggage into a hotel for myself." The chin went a notch higher in the air and Amelia fixed her gaze on Logan's amused expression. "Perhaps Mr. Reed needs assistance with *his* things."

Jeffery looked from Amelia's stern expression to Logan's near laughing one. Appearing confused, he neither offered his assistance to Logan, nor did he protest when Amelia went off in the direction of the hotel, bags in hand.

The St. Vrain Hotel was no cooler inside than it had been outside. If anything it was even more stifling because there was no breeze and the flies were thicker here than in the streets. She turned at the front desk to await her father and struggled to contain a smile when he and Mattersley appeared, each with his own bags, and her sisters struggling dramatically behind them.

"Oh, Papa," Margaret moaned loudly, "you simply cannot expect me to carry all of this!" the earl rolled his eyes, bringing a broad smile from Amelia. The clerk at the desk also seemed amused, but said nothing. Amelia was thankful Logan Reed was still outside with the horses.

Jeffery strode in, trying hard to look completely at ease with his new task. He put his things down in one corner and announced he would go with Mr. Reed to stable the horses. Amelia was stunned by this. So far as she knew, Jeffery had done nothing more than hand his horse over for stabling since his privileged childhood. How she would love to watch him in the livery with Mr. Reed!

Amelia gave it no more thought, however, as the clerk led them upstairs to their rooms. She would share a room with her sisters again, but this time there were two beds. One was a rustic-looking, double-sized bed. It looked roughly hewn from pine, yet a colorful handmade quilt made it appear beautiful. The other, a single bed, looked to be even more crudely assembled. It, too, was covered with a multi-colored quilt, and to the exhausted Amelia, looked quite satisfactory. Other than the beds, the room was rather empty. There was a single night table with a bowl and pitcher of water and a tiny closet that was hardly big enough to hang a single dress within.

"Oh, such misery!" Penelope exclaimed and Margaret quickly agreed.

"How could Papa make us stay in a horrible place like this?" Margaret added.

"I think it will seem a great deal more appealing after you've spent two or three nights on the trail," Amelia said without asking her sisters' permission to take the single bed. She tossed her things to the floor and stretched out on top of the quilt, still dressed in her dusty clothes.

The bed isn't half bad, Amelia thought. *It beats being on the back of that temperamental mount Mr. Reed had insisted she ride.* Twice the beast had tried to take his own head and leave the processional, but Amelia, seasoned rider that she was, gave the gelding beneath her a firm understanding that she was to decide the way, not he. No doubt Mr. Reed had intentionally given her the spirited horse. *He probably hoped to find me sprawled out on the prairie ground,* she mused. *I guess I showed him that I can handle my own affairs.* It was the last conscious thought Amelia had for some time.

❧

She had no idea how long she'd laid upon the bed. Her sisters had been arguing about who would sleep on the right side of the bed and who would go to search out another veiled bonnet. The noise was something she was used to—it was the silence which seemed to awaken her. Staring at the ceiling for a moment, Amelia tried to remember where she was and what she was to do next. She had no time for further contemplation, however, when a knock sounded at her door.

"Yes?" she questioned, barely cracking the door open.

A young woman wearing a starched white apron stood before her bearing a towel and bar of soap. "We've a bath ready for you, Lady Amhurst."

No announcement could have met with her approval more. Amelia opened the door wide and grimaced at the stiffness that was already setting into her bones. It had been a while since she'd been riding, what with the boat ride to America and the constant use of trains and stages thereafter.

"Thank you. Will you direct me?"

The woman, hardly old enough to be called that, motioned Amelia to the room at the end of the hall. "I can get you settled in and take your clothes to have the dust beaten out. I'll bring you something else to wear if you tell me what you want."

Amelia stepped into the room and thought the steaming

b of water too good to be true. She immediately began
nfastening the buttons of her half jacket. "You are very
ind to arrange all of this for me. I must say the service here
s quite good."

"Oh, it's my job," the girl replied. " 'Sides, Logan told me
ou'd probably want to clean up and he gave me an extra
oin to make sure you were taken care of personally."

Amelia's fingers ceased at their task. "I beg your pardon?
Mr. Reed paid for this bath?"

"Yes, ma'am."

Amelia hesitated, looked at the tub and considered her
pride in the matter. The steaming water beckoned her and her
tired limbs pleaded for the refreshment. She could always
settle things with Logan Reed later.

"Very well." She slipped out of the jacket and unbuttoned
her skirt. "If you'll bring me my black skirt and a clean
shirtwaist, I'll wash out these other things." She would show
Mr. Reed just how self-sufficient she could be.

"Oh no, ma'am. I can take care of everything for you. My
mother does the laundry and she can have these things ready
by morning. Pressed fresh and smelling sweet. You'll see."

Amelia reluctantly gave in. "Very well." She sent the girl
off with her riding clothes, keeping only her camisole and
bloomers. These she washed out by hand and hung to dry
before stepping into the tub. With the window open to allow
in the breeze, the items would dry by the time she finished
with the bath. That was one of the nice things about the drier
air of Colorado. Things took forever to dry back home in
England. The dampness was nearly always with them and it
was better to press clothes dry with an iron than wait for
them to dry on their own. But here the air was crisp and dry
and even in the heat of the day it was completely tolerable
compared to what she'd endured when they visited a very
humid New Orleans.

Sinking into the hot water, Amelia sighed aloud. How good it felt! Her dry skin seemed to literally drink in the offered moisture. Lathering the soap down one arm and then the other, Amelia wanted to cry with relief. The bath was pure pleasure and she felt like the spoiled aristocrat Logan Reed thought her to be. After washing thoroughly, she eased back on the rim of the tub and let the water come up to her neck, soothing and easing all the pain in her shoulders. It mattered very little that Logan Reed had arranged this luxury. At that moment, the only thing that mattered was the comfort at hand.

When the knock on the door sounded, Amelia realized she'd dozed off again. The water was tepid now and her muscles were no longer sore and tense.

"It's me, Lady Amhurst," the voice of the young woman called. "I've brought your clothes."

"Come ahead," Amelia called, stepping from the tub to wrap the rough towel around her body.

The girl appeared bringing not only the requested skirt and shirtwaist, but Amelia's comb and brush. "I thought you might be needin' these too. I can help with your hair, if you like."

Amelia smiled. What a friendly little thing. She'd make a good chambermaid if she were a little less familiar. But that was the way of these Americans and Amelia found herself growing more accepting of it as the days wore on. To be friendly and openly honest was not a thing one could count on in the finer classes of people. Women of high society were taught to keep their opinions to themselves, and in fact, were encouraged to have no opinion at all. From the moment she was born, Amelia was strictly lectured that her father, and later her husband, would clearly do her thinking for her. Amelia had other ideas, however, and often she came off appearing smug and superior in her attitudes.

People misjudged her confidence and believed her to think herself better than her peers. But it wasn't true.

Logan Reed came to mind. He, too, had misjudged her and her kind. Americans seemed more than happy to lend their opinion to a situation. Even this young woman gave her opinion at every turn. But, where Logan had made her feel quite the snob, this young woman made her feel like royalty. Then a thought crossed her mind and she frowned. "Did Mr. Reed pay for you to assist me with my hair as well?"

"Oh, no, ma'am. I was just thinking you might want some help what with it coming down in back and all. I can't do it up fancy like you had it, but I can help pin it up."

Amelia nodded. "Yes, I'd like that very much." The girl turned away while Amelia stepped into her underthings. They were a little damp and this seemed to make them cooler. Light was fading outside and Amelia knew it must nearly be dinner time. These Americans had the barbaric custom of eating a full meal not long after the time when she was more accustomed to tea and cakes. Supper at home was always an affair to dress for and always served late into the evening—sometimes even after nine. *Alas, yet another American custom to adapt to.*

The girl instructed Amelia to sit on a stool while she combed out the thick, waist-length tresses. Amelia prided herself on her hair. It was a light, golden blond which most all of her peers envied. To be both blond-headed and blue-eyed in her society, was to be the picture of perfection. Added to this was her, *how did Mr. Reed say it?* robust figure. Amelia smiled to herself. Many a glance had come to her by gentlemen too well-bred to say what Logan Reed had issued without the slightest embarrassment. She was robust, or voluptuous as her dear friend Sarah would say. When corseted tightly, she had a perfect hour-glass figure, well nearly perfect. Maybe time ran a little heavier on the top half than the bottom.

"There, how's that?"

Amelia took the offered mirror and smiled. The young woman had done a fine job of replicating her earlier coiffure. "It's exactly right, Miss. . ."

"Oh, just call me Emma."

"Well, thank you very much Emma." Amelia got to her feet and allowed Emma to help her dress. "Are the others going to bathe?"

"Oh, the menfolk went down to the steambath at the barbershop. The other womenfolk didn't seem to take kindly to my trying to offer up help, so I pretty much left them alone."

Amelia nodded and smiled. She could well imagine her sisters' snobbery keeping them from accepting the assistance of this young woman. And no doubt, Lady Gambett and her pouty brood had taken themselves off to a private wash basin. With a final pat to her hair, Amelia gathered up her things and followed Emma from the room. "You should see my father, Lord Amhurst, for the cost of this bath and my clothing being cleaned. Mr. Reed is no more than a hunting guide to our party and certainly has no call to be arranging my affairs."

Emma smiled. "Oh, that's just Logan's way. He's friendly like that."

"Well, I assure you I am not in the habit of allowing strangers, especially men, to be friendly like that with me. Please see my father with the bill."

❧

Supper that evening was a surprisingly pleasant fare of roasted chicken, sage dressing, a veritable banquet of vegetables—mostly canned, but very tasty, and peach cobbler. Amelia had to admit it was more than she'd expected and only the thick swarm of hovering black flies kept her from completely enjoying her evening. That and Logan Reed's rude appraisal of her throughout the meal. He seemed to watch her as though she might steal the silver at any given moment. Amelia grew increasingly uncomfortable under his scrutiny until she actually found herself listening to Sir Jeffery's soliloquy on the founding of the London Medical School for Women and the obsurdity of anyone believing women would make acceptable physicians.

"Why the very thought of exposing the gentler sex to such grotesqueries is quite abominable," Jeffery stated as though that would be the collective reasoning of the entire party.

Normally Amelia would have commented loud and clear on such outdated thoughts, but with Logan apparently anticipating such a scene, she chose instead to finish her meal and quietly excuse herself. This was accomplished without much ado, mainly because Lady Gambett opened the matter and excused herself first, pleading an intolerable headache.

Amelia soon followed suit and very nearly spilled over a water glass when she got to her feet. Her hands were shaking as she righted the glass. Looking up, she found Logan smiling. She had to get away from him quickly or make a complete fool of herself, of this she was certain.

Unfortunately, she was barely out the front door when Jeffery popped up at her side.

"Ah, Sir Jeffery," she said stiffly.

"Good evening, Lady Amhurst," he said, pausing with a smile, "Amelia."

She stiffened even more. Eyeing him with complete contempt she said nothing. There was no need. She'd often heard it said that with a single look she could freeze the heart right out of a man and Jeffery Chamberlain was certainly no match for her.

"Forgive me, Lady Amhurst," he said bowing low before her. "I sought only to escort you to wherever it is you might be going. The familiarity is born only out of my fondness for you and your good father's desire that we wed."

Amelia nodded. "You may be assured that those desires reside with my father alone. Good evening." She hurried away before Jeffery could respond. She hadn't the strength to discuss the matter further.

The evening had grown quite chilly and Amelia was instantly sorry she'd not stopped to retrieve a shawl. She was grateful for the short-waisted jacket she'd donned for dinner and quickly did up the remaining two buttons to insure as much warmth as possible. After two blocks, however, she was more than happy to head back to the hotel and remain within its thin walls until morning sent them ever upward.

Upward.

She glanced to the now blackened images of the mountain range before her. The shadows seemed foreboding, as if some great hulking monster waited to devour her. Shuddering from the thought, she walked back to the St. Vrain Hotel and considered it no more.

four

It was the wind that woke Amelia in the morning. The great wailing gusts bore down from the mountains causing the very timbers around her to shake and tremble. *Was it a storm?* She contemplated this for a moment, hoping that if it were, it would rain and drown out each and every pesky fly in Longmont. All through the night, her sleep had been disturbed by the constant assault of flies at her face, in her hair, and at her ears. It was enough to make her consider agreeing to marry Jeffery if her father would pledge to return immediately to England.

A light rapping sounded upon her door. Amelia pulled the blanket tight around her shoulders and went to answer it.

"Yes?" she called, stumbling in the dark.

"It's me, Emma."

Amelia opened the door with a sleepy nod. "Are we about to blow away?"

Emma laughed softly and pushed past Amelia to light the lamp on her night table. "Oh, no, ma'am. The wind blows like this from time to time. It'll probably be done by breakfast. Mr. Reed sent me to wake you and the other ladies. Said to tell you it was an hour before dawn and you'd know exactly what that meant."

Amelia frowned. "Yes, indeed. Thank you, Emma."

"Will you be needin' help with your hair and gettin' dressed?"

"No, thank you anyway. Mr. Reed made it quite clear that simplicity is the means for success on this excursion. I intend only to braid my hair and pin it tight. From the sound

39

of the wind, I suppose I should pin it very tight." Emma giggled and Amelia smiled in spite of herself. *Perhaps some of these Americans aren't so bad.*

"Lady Gambett was near to tears last night because Logan told her that she and those youngun's of hers needed to get rid of their corsets before they rode another ten feet."

It was Amelia's turn to giggle. Something she'd not done in years. "Surely you jest."

"Jest?" Emma looked puzzled.

"Joke. I merely implied that you were surely joking."

"Oh, no! He said it. I heard him."

"Well, I've never been one to abide gossip," Amelia began rather soberly, "but I can well imagine the look on Lady Gambett's face when he mentioned the unmentionable item."

"She plumb turned red and called for her smelling salts."

"Yes, she would."

Glancing to where Penelope and Margaret continued to slumber soundly, Emma questioned, "Will you need me to wake your sisters?"

Amelia glanced at the bed. "No, it would take more than your light touch. I'll see to them." Emma smiled and took her leave.

"Wake up sleepyheads," Amelia said, pulling the quilts to the foot of the bed. Penelope shrieked a protest and pulled them back up, while Margaret stared up in disbelief.

"I believe you're becoming as ill-mannered as these Americans," she said to Amelia.

"It's still dark outside," Penelope added, snuggling down. "Mr. Reed said we start at dawn."

"Mr. Reed said we leave at dawn," she reminded them. "I for one intend to have enough time to dress properly and eat before climbing back on that ill-tempered horse."

Margaret whined. "We are too tired to bother with eating. Just go away, Amelia."

"Have it your way," Amelia said with a shrug. And with that she left her sisters to worry about themselves, and hurried to dress for the day. Pulling on black cotton stockings, pantaloons and camisole, Amelia smiled privately, knowing that she was quite glad for the excuse to be rid of her corset. She packed the corset away, all the while feeling quite smug. She wasn't about to give Logan Reed a chance to speak so forwardly to her about things which didn't concern him. Pulling on her riding outfit, now clean and pressed, she secured her toiletries in her saddlebags and hurried to meet the others at breakfast.

Much to her embarrassment she arrived to find herself alone with Logan. The rest of her party was slow to rise and even slower to ready themselves for the day ahead. Logan nodded approvingly at her and called for the meal to be served. He bowed ever so slightly and held out a chair for Amelia.

"We must wait for the others, Mr. Reed," she said, taking the offered seat.

"I'm afraid we can't," Logan announced. "You forget I'm experienced at this. Most folks refuse to take me seriously until they miss at least one breakfast. Ahhh, here's Emma." The young girl entered bringing a mound of biscuits—complete with hovering flies—and a platter of fried sausages swimming in grease and heavily peppered. It was only after taking one of the offered links that Amelia realized it wasn't pepper at all, but still more flies.

Frowning at the food on her plate, it was as if Logan read her mind when he said, "Just try to think of 'em as extra meat."

Amelia almost smiled, but refused to. "Maybe I'll just eat a biscuit."

"You'd best eat up and eat well. The mountain air will make you feel starved and after all the hard work you'll be doing, you'll wish you'd had more than biscuits."

"Hard work?"

Logan waited to speak until Emma brought two more platters, one with eggs, another with fried potatoes, and a bowl with thick white gravy. He thanked the girl and turned to Amelia. "Shall we say grace?"

"I hardly think so, Mr. Reed. To whom should we offer thanks, except to those whose hands have provided and prepared the food?"

For the first time since she'd met the smug, self-confident Logan Reed, he stared at her speechless and dumbstruck. *Good,* she thought. *Let him consider that matter for a time and leave me to eat in silence.* She put eggs on her plate and added a heavy amount of cream to the horrible black coffee Emma had poured into her cup. She longed to plead with the girl for tea, but wouldn't think of allowing Mr. Reed to see her in a weakened moment.

"Do you mean to tell me," Logan began, "that you don't believe in God?"

Amelia didn't even look up. "Indeed, that is precisely what I mean to say."

"How can a person who seems to be of at least average intelligence," at this Amelia's head snapped up and Logan chuckled and continued, "I thought that might get your attention. How can you look around you or wake up in the morning to breathe the air of a new day and believe there is no God?"

Amelia scowled at the black flies hovering around her fork. "Should there have been a God, surely He would not have allowed such imperfect creatures to mar His universe."

"You don't believe in God because flies are sharing your breakfast table?" Logan's expression was one of complete confusion. He hadn't even started to eat his own food.

"Mr. Reed, I believe this trip will go a great deal better for both of us if you will merely mind your own business and leave me to do the same. I fail to see where my disbelief in a supreme being is of any concern to you, and therefore, I see no reason to discuss the matter further."

Logan hesitated for a moment, bowed his head to what Amelia presumed were his prayers of grace, and ate in silence for several minutes. For some reason, even though it was exactly what Amelia had hoped for, she felt uncomfortable and found herself wishing he would say something even if it were to insult her.

When he continued in silence, she played at eating the breakfast. She'd hoped the wind would send the flies further down the prairie, but it only seemed to have driven them indoors for shelter. As the gales died down outside, she could only hope they'd seek new territory.

"I guess I see it as my business to concern myself with the eternal souls of mankind," Logan said without warning. "See the Bible, that's the Word of God. . ."

"I know what the Bible is perceived to be, Mr. Reed. I wasn't born without a brain, simply without the need for an all-interfering, all-powerful being."

Logan seemed to shake this off before continuing. His green eyes seemed to darken. "The Bible says we are to concern ourselves with our fellow man and spread the good news."

She put her fork down and matched his look of determination. "And pray tell, Mr. Reed, what would that good news be? Spread it quickly and leave me to my meal." Amelia knew she was being unreasonably harsh, but she tired of religious rhetoric and nonsensical sermons. She'd long given up the farce of accompanying her sisters and father to church, knowing that they no more held the idea of worshipping as a holy matter than did she.

"The good news is that folks like you and I don't have to burn in the pits of hell for all eternity, because Jesus Christ, God's only son, came to live and die for our sins. He rose again, to show that death cannot hold the Christian from eternal life."

Amelia picked up her thick white mug and sipped the steaming contents. The coffee scalded her all the way down, but she'd just as soon admit to the pain as to admit Logan's words were having any affect on her whatsoever. *The pits of hell, indeed,* she thought.

She tried to compose herself before picking the fork up again. "I believe religion to be man's way of comforting himself in the face of death. Mankind can simply not bear to imagine that there is only so much time allotted to each person so mankind has created religion to support the idea of there being something more. The Hindu believe we are reincarnated. Incarnate is from the Latin *incarnates,* meaning made flesh. So they believe much as you Christians do that they will rise up to live again."

"I know what reincarnation means, and I am even familiar with the Hindu religion. But you're completely wrong when you say they believe as Christians do. They don't hold faith in what Jesus did to save us. They don't believe in the need for salvation through Him in order to have that eternal life."

Amelia shrugged. "To each religion and culture comes a theory that will comfort them the most. In light of that, Mr. Reed, and considering the hundreds of different religions in the world, even the varied philosophies within your own Christian faith, how can you possibly ascertain that you and you alone, have the one true faith?"

"Are you saying that there is no need for faith *and* that there is no such thing as God?" Logan countered.

"I am a woman of intellect and reason, Mr. Reed. Intellectually and reasonably, I assure you that faith and religion have no physical basis for belief."

"Faith in God is just that, Lady Amhurst. Faith." Logan slammed down his coffee mug. "I am a man of intellect and reason, but it only makes it that much clearer to me that there is a need for God and something more than the contrivances of mankind."

Amelia looked at him for a moment. *Yes, I could believe this barbaric American might have some understanding of books and philosophies. But he is still of that mind set which uses religion as a crutch to ease his conscience and concerns.* Before Amelia could comment further, Logan got to his feet and stuffed two more biscuits into the pocket of his brown flannel shirt. Amelia appraised him silently as he thanked Emma for a great meal and pulled on his drifters coat.

"We leave in ten minutes. I'll bring the horses around to the front." He stalked out of the room like a man with a great deal on his mind, leaving Amelia feeling as though she'd had a bit of a comeuppance, but for the life of her she couldn't quite figure out just how he'd done it.

Emma cleared Logan's plate and mug from the table and returned to find Amelia staring silently at the void left by their guide.

"I hate to be a busybody, Lady Amhurst," Emma began, "but your family ain't a bit concerned about Mr. Reed's timetable and I can tell you from experience, Logan won't wait."

This brought Amelia's attention instantly. "I'll tend to them. Are there more of these biscuits?"

"Yes, ma'am."

"Good. Please pack whatever of this breakfast you can for us and we'll take it along. As I recall, Mr. Reed said there would be a good six miles of prairie to cross to the canyon."

"I can wrap the biscuits and sausage into a cloth, but the rest of this won't pack very good."

Amelia blotted her lips with a coarse napkin and got to her feet. "Do what you can, Emma, and I'll retrieve my wayward family."

Ten minutes later, Amelia had managed to see her family to the front of the hotel. Penelope and Margaret were whining, still struggling to do something with their hair. Upon Amelia's threat to shear them both they grew instantly silent. Lady Gambett cried softly into a lace-edged handkerchief and bemoaned the fact that her nerves would never stand the jostling on horseback. Her daughters were awkward and consciously concerned about their lack of corseting, and Amelia had to laugh when she overheard Margaret tell Josephine that Mr. Reed was no doubt some kind of devious man who would do them all in once they were far enough away from the protection of town. A part of Amelia was beginning to understand Logan Reed's misgivings about her people.

Logan repacked the mules with the baggage and items brought to him by the party, but Amelia noticed he was unusually tight-lipped. Light was just streaking the eastern skies when he hauled up onto the back of his horse and instructed them to do the same.

Amelia allowed Jeffery to help her onto her horse and winced noticeably when the softer parts of her body protested from the abuse she'd inflicted the day before. She said nothing, noting Logan's smirk of recognition, but her sisters and the Gambetts were well into moans and protests of discomfort. Logan ignored them all, however, and urged his horse and the mules forward.

❧

It wasn't yet ten o'clock when Logan first heard Amelia's sisters suggesting they stop. He couldn't help but cast a smug look of satisfaction toward Amelia when Penelope suggested they should imbibe in a time of tea and cakes.

He watched Amelia's face grow flush with embarrassment, but she said nothing, choosing instead to let her mount lag behind the others until she was nearly bringing up the rear of the party. Chuckling to himself, Logan led them on another two hours before finally drawing his horse to a stop.

Dismounting, he called over his shoulder, "We'll take lunch here."

It was as if the entire party sighed in unison.

Logan quickly set up everything they would need. He drew cold water from the mountain river which they'd followed through the canyon, then dug around in the saddlebags to produce jerked beef and additional biscuits.

"You surely don't mean this to be our luncheon fare," Jeffery Chamberlain said in complete disgust.

The earl looked down his nose at the pitiful offering. "Yes, Mr. Reed, surely there is something better than this."

Logan pushed his hat back on his head. "We'll have a hot meal for dinner this evening. If we're to push ahead and reach our first camping point before dark, we'll only have time to rest here about ten, maybe fifteen minutes. It'll give the horses a well-deserved break and allow them to water up. The higher we go the more water you'll need to drink. Remember that and you won't find yourself succumbing to sorche."

"I beg your pardon?" Lord Amhurst questioned.

"Mountain sickness," Reed stated flatly. "The air is much thinner up here, but since you've traipsed all over the Alps, you should already know all about that. You need to take it slower and allow yourselves time to get used to the altitude. Otherwise, you'll be losing what little lunch you get and dealing with eye splitting headaches that won't let you go for weeks. It's one more reason I insisted the ladies dismiss the idea of corsets." Shudders and gasps of indignant shock echoed from the now gathered Gambett and Amhurst women. With exception of Amelia. She stood to one side admiring a collection of wildflowers, but Logan knew she was listening by the amused expression on her face.

Logan continued, trying hard to ignore the graceful blond

as she moved about the river bank studying the ground. "As inappropriate as you might think my addressing the subject of women's undergarments might be, it is a matter of life and death. Up here beauty is counted in the scenery, not the flesh. The air is thinner and you need more of it to account for what you're used to breathing down below. Losing those corsets just might save your life. I wouldn't even suggest putting them back on after we arrive in Estes. The altitude there is even higher than it is here and I'd sure hate to have to run around all day picking up women in dead faints. Now I've wasted enough time. Eat or don't, the choice is yours. I'll water the horses and mules while you decide." He started to walk away then turned back. "I hate to approach another delicate subject, but should you take yourself off into the trees for privacy, keep your eyes open. I'd also hate to have to deal with an agitated mother bear just because you startled her while she was feeding her cubs."

With that said, he walked away grumbling to himself. These prim and proper Brits were more trouble to deal with than they were worth. This was the last time he'd ever act as guide for anyone of English nobility.

He tethered his horse at the riverbank and pretended to adjust the saddle while he watched Amelia picking flowers and studying them with an almost scientific eye. From time to time, she drew out a small book and pressed one of these samples between the pages, before moving on to the next point of interest. He found himself admiring the way she lithely climbed over the rocks and couldn't help but notice her lack of fear as she neared the rushing river for a closer look.

As she held a leaf up to catch the sunlight, Logan was reminded of her atheistic views. *How could anyone behold the beauty of this canyon and question the existence of God?* It was one thing not to want to deal with God, or even to question whether He truly cared to deal with mankind, but to openly declare there to be no God—that was something he couldn't even fathom. Even the Indians he'd dealt with believed in God. Maybe they didn't believe the same way he did, but they didn't question that someone or something greater than man held the universe in order and sustained life.

Logan tried not to stare at Amelia, but he found himself rather helpless to ignore her. The other women were huddled together relaying their misfortunes, hoping for better times ahead and assuring each other that such torture could be endured for the sake of their menfolk. The men were gingerly sampling the lunch fare and after deciding it was better than nothing, they managed to eat a good portion before convincing the women to partake.

Logan wondered if Amelia would partake, but then he saw her draw a biscuit from the deep pocket of her skirt and nibble at it absentmindedly as she bent to pick up a piece of granite. *She is an industrious woman,* he thought, watching her turn the stone in her hand. *Who else could have gotten that sour-faced brood of travelers together in such a short time? Who else too, would have thought to get Emma to pack food for them to take, rather than whine and beg him to allow them a bit more time for breakfast?*

As if sensing his gaze upon her, Amelia looked up and met his stare. Neither one did anything for a moment and when Amelia returned her attention to the rock, Logan tried to focus on the mules. His stomach did a bit of a flip-flop and he smiled in spite of himself at the affect this woman was having on him. Stealing a sidelong glance he watched her cup water from the river's edge and drink. *Yes, Lady Amhurst is quite a woman.*

"We'll be leaving in a few minutes," Logan announced to the weary band. "Take care of your needs before that." He walked to where Amelia sat quietly contemplating the scenery. "It's impressive, don't you think?" he asked, wondering if she'd take offense.

"Yes, it is," she admitted.

"Those are cottonwood trees," he said pointing out tall green-leaved trees. "Those with the lighter bark are aspen." He reached down and picked up a leaf. "This is an aspen leaf." Amelia seemed interested enough and so he continued. "I noticed you were saving flowers and if you need any help in identifying them later, I'd be happy to be of service. I'm pretty knowledgeable about the vegetation and wildlife in these parts." He tried to sound nonchalant for fear he'd frighten her away or anger her.

"I especially like those blue flowers," Amelia replied.

"Those are columbine. ' 'Tis said that absence conquers love! But, O, believe it not; I've tried alas! its power to prove, But thou art not forgot.' A fellow named F. W. Thomas wrote that. It's from a poem called 'The Columbine'."

"How interesting." She said nothing more for a moment, then added, "What of those white ones with the short hairy stems?"

"Pasqueflowers. So named because they usually start flowering around Easter time. Comes from the Latin word *pascha* or the Hebrew *pesah* meaning 'a passing over', thus the Jewish feast of Passover and the Christian celebration of Easter, the death and resurrection of Christ." He really hadn't intended it as a mocking to Amelia's earlier lessons on *incarnate*, but even as the words left his mouth, he knew that was what they'd sound like.

Amelia stiffened, picked up her things and walked back to the horse without another word. Logan wanted to kick himself for breaking the brief civil respite from the tension between them. *Sometimes, Reed,* he thought, *you can sure put your foot in your mouth.*

five

Amelia tried not to remember the way Logan Reed had stared at her. Or how green his eyes were. Or how his mustache twitched whenever he was trying not to smile. She found herself unwillingly drawn to him and the very thought disturbed her to the bone. He was refreshingly different from English gentlemen and far better mannered than she'd given him credit for. His gruff exterior was mostly show, she'd decided while watching him help Lady Gambett onto her horse. He had tipped his hat and said something which had caused Lady Gambett to actually smile. Keeping these thoughts to herself, Amelia concentrated on the scenery around her.

"You are particularly quiet," Jeffery spoke, riding up alongside her. It was one of those rare places along the path that allowed for riders to go two abreast.

"I'm considering the countryside," she replied rather tightly.

"Ah, yes. America and her rough-hewn beauty."

Amelia frowned. "And what, pray tell, is that supposed to mean?"

Jeffery smiled tolerantly. "Simply that I'll be happy to return home to England. I'll be even happier when you reconcile yourself to our union and allow me to properly court you."

"I do not wish to discuss the matter."

"I know that very well, but I also know it is your father's intentions that we do so."

He lifted his face to catch a bit of the sun's warmth and

Amelia was reminded of a turkey stretching his neck. *Perhaps he might let out a gobble at any moment.* She chuckled in spite of her resolve to be firm.

Jeffery lowered his head and stared at her soberly. "Have I somehow amused you?"

Amelia shook her head. "No, not really. I'm just a bit giddy from the thin air. I'm sure you will understand if I wish to save my breath and discontinue our conversation." She urged her horse ahead and was relieved when Jeffery chose to leave her alone.

❧

Their stop for the evening came early. The sun was just disappearing behind the snow-capped peaks in front of them when Lord Amhurst's pocket watch read 3:35. Amelia slid down from the horse and stretched in a rather unladylike display. Margaret gasped and Penelope laughed, while the Gambett women were too intent on their own miseries to notice. Amelia shrugged off her sisters' questioning stares and began pulling her bedroll free from behind the saddle.

"Get your horses cared for first," Logan called out. "Take down your things and I'll come around and take care of the saddles and staking the animals out."

Moans arose from the crowd and Amelia wasn't sure but what even Mattersley was echoing the sentiment of the group. The older man looked quite worn and Amelia felt concern for him. He would die before leaving her father's side, and thus, he accompanied them whenever they traveled. But this time the trip was so much rougher. Amelia wondered if he would be able to meet the demands of the American wilderness.

"You did good today," Logan said, taking the reins of her mount. "If you think you're up to it, I could use some help putting up the tents and getting dinner started."

Amelia nodded and for some reason she felt honored that

he'd asked for her assistance. While Logan removed saddles, Amelia went to Mattersley and helped him remove his bedroll. She didn't know why she acted in such a manner, but felt amply rewarded when Mattersley gave her a brief, rare smile. She took his mount and led it to where Logan was staking out Lady Gambett's mount.

"I see you're getting into the spirit of things," Logan said, quickly uncinching the horse.

"I'm worried about Mattersley. He doesn't seem to be adapting well to the altitude." Amelia looked beyond the horses to where Mattersley was trying to assist her father. "He won't be parted from my father," she added, as though Logan had asked her why the old man was along. "He is completely devoted to him."

"I can't imagine what it'd be like to have someone devoted to you like that," Logan replied softly.

Amelia looked into his eyes and found him completely serious. "Me either," she murmured. He made her feel suddenly very vulnerable, even lonely.

Logan's green eyes seemed to break through the thinly placed wall of English aristocracy, to gaze inside to where Amelia knew her empty heart beat a little faster. *Could he really see through her and find the void within that kept her so distant and uncomfortable?*

"My mother was devoted to my pa that way," he added in a barely audible voice.

Amelia nodded. "Mine too. When she died, I think of a part of him died as well. There is a great deal of pain in realizing that you've lost something forever."

"It doesn't have to be forever," Logan said, refusing to break his stare.

Amelia licked her dry lips nervously. "No?"

"No. That's one of the nice things about God and it isn't just a theory to give you comfort when somebody dies. If you and your loved ones belong to Him, then you will see them again."

Amelia swallowed hard. For the first time in many years, in fact since her mother's death, she felt an aching urge to cry for her loss. "My mother believed that way," she murmured.

Logan's face brightened. "Then half the problem is solved. She's in heaven just waiting for you to figure out that she knew what she was talking about. You can see her again."

Amelia's sorrow faded into prideful scorn. "My mother is entombed in the family mausoleum and I have no desire to see her again." She walked away quickly, feeling Logan's gaze on her. *How dare he intrude into my life like that? How dare he trespass in the privacy of my soul?*

❧

"Come on," Logan said several minutes later. He tossed a small mallet at Amelia's feet and motioned her to follow him.

Picking up the mallet, Amelia did as she was told. She wasn't surprised when she found Logan quite serious about her helping him assemble tents. He laid out the canvas structures and showed her where to drive the stakes into the ground. Pounding the wooden stakes caused her teeth to rattle, but Amelia found herself attacking the job with a fury.

Logan secured the tent poles and pulled the structure tight. To Amelia's surprise and pleasure, an instant shelter was born. Two more structures went up without a single mishap, or word spoken between them. Amelia was panting by the time they'd finished, but she didn't care.

Logan had sent the others to gather wood, but their production was minimal at best. When he and Amelia had finished with the tents, he then instructed the weary entourage to take their things into the tents.

"The ladies will have two tents and the men can use the other. It'll be a close fit, but by morning you'll be glad to rug up with the other occupants."

No one said a word.

Amelia took her things to the tent and started to unroll her bedding. "Leave it rolled," Logan instructed from behind her.

"I beg your pardon?" She pushed back an errant strand of hair and straightened up.

"Unrolled, it will draw moisture or critters. Wait until you're ready to sleep."

Amelia nodded. "Very well. What would you like me to do now?"

"We're going to get dinner going. Hungry?"

She smiled weakly. "Famished." In truth, she was not only hungry but light-headed.

"Come along then," he said in a rather fatherly tone. "I'll show you how to make camp stew."

"Camp stew?" she said, concentrating on his words against the pulsating beat of her heart in her ears.

He grinned. "Camp stew is going to be our primary feast while en route to your summer home. It's just a fancy way of saying beans and dried beef. Sometimes I throw in a few potatoes just to break the monotony."

Amelia allowed herself to smile. "At this point it sounds like a feast."

"You can take this to the river and get some water," he said, handing her a coffee pot. "I'll unpack the pot for the beans. You'll need to fill it with water first, then bring the coffee pot back full and we'll make some coffee."

She nodded wearily and made her way to the water's edge. Her head was beginning to ache and a voice from within reminded her of Mr. Reed's warning to drink plenty of water. Scooping a handful to her lips, Amelia thought she'd never tasted anything as good. The water was cold and clear and instantly refreshed her. With each return trip Amelia forced herself to drink a little water. On her last trip, she dipped her handkerchief in the icy river and wiped some of the grime away from her face. She drew in gasping breaths of chilled mountain air, trying hard to compensate for the lack of oxygen. For a moment the world seemed to spin.

Lowering her gaze, Amelia panicked at the sensation of dizziness. It seemed to come in waves, leaving her unable to focus. She took a step and stumbled. Took another and nearly fell over backward. *What's happening to me?* she worried.

"Amelia?" Logan was calling from somewhere. "You got that coffee water yet?"

The river was situated far enough away that the trees and rocks kept her from view of the camp. She opened her mouth to call out, then clamped it shut, determined not to ask Mr. Reed for help. Sliding down to sit on a small boulder, Amelia steadied the pot. *I'll feel better in a minute,* she thought. *If I just sit for a moment, everything will clear and I'll have my breath back.*

"Amelia?" Logan stood not three feet away. "Are you all right?"

Getting to her feet quickly, Amelia instantly realized her mistake. The coffee pot fell with a clatter against the rocks and Amelia felt her knees buckle.

"Whoa, there," Logan said, reaching out to catch her before she hit the ground. "I was afraid you were doing too much. You are the most prideful, stubborn woman I've ever met."

Amelia tried to push him away and stand on her own, but her head and legs refused to work together and her hands only seemed to flail at the air. "I just got up too fast," she protested.

"You just managed to get yourself overworked. You're going to lay down for the rest of the night. I'll bring you some chow when it's ready, but 'til then, you aren't to lift a finger." In one fluid motion he swung her up into his arms.

"I assure you, Mr. Reed—"

"Logan. My name is Logan. Just as you are Lady Amhurst, I am Logan. Understand?" he sounded gruff, but he was smiling and Amelia could only laugh. She'd brought this on herself by trying to outdo the others and keep up with any task he'd suggested.

"Well?" His eyes seemed to twinkle.

"I understand!" she declared and tried not to notice the feel of his muscular arms around her.

His expression sobered and Amelia couldn't help but notice that there was no twitching of that magnificent mustache. Sometimes, just sometimes, she wondered what it would be like to touch that mustache. *Is it coarse and prickly, or smooth and soft like the pet rabbit Margaret had played with as a child?*

He was looking at her as though trying to say something that couldn't be formed into words and for once, Amelia didn't think him so barbaric. These new considerations of a man she'd once thought hopelessly crude, were disturbing to her. Her mind began to race. *What should I say to him? What should I do? I could demand he release me, but I seriously doubt he would. And what if he did? Did she really want that?*

This is ridiculous, she chided herself. Forcing her gaze to the path, she nodded and said, "Shouldn't we get back? Maybe you could just put me down now. I'm feeling much better."

Logan gave her a little toss upward to get a better hold. She let out an audible gasp and tightly gripped her arms around Logan's neck.

"Don't!" she squealed with the abandonment of a child. Logan looked at her strangely and Amelia tried to calm her nerves. "I— I've always been afraid of falling," she offered lamely. "Please put me down."

"Nope," he said and started for camp. When he came to the edge of the clearing it was evident that everyone else was still collecting firewood. Logan stopped and asked, "Why are you afraid of falling?"

Amelia's mind went back in time. "When I was very young someone held me out over the edge of the balcony and threatened to spill me. I was absolutely terrified and engaged myself in quite a spell until Mother reprimanded me for being so loud."

"No reprimand for the one doing the teasing, eh?" Logan's voice was soft and sympathetic.

"No, she knew Jeffery didn't mean anything by it." Amelia could have laughed at the stunned expression on Logan's face.

"Not, Sir Jeffery?" he asked in mock horror.

"None other. I think it amused him to see me weak and helpless."

"Then he's a twit."

Amelia's grin broadened into a smile. "Yes, he is."

"Amelia! What's wrong!"

"Speaking of the twit," Logan growled low against her ear and Amelia giggled. His warm breath against her ear, not to mention the mustache, tickled. "Amelia's fine, she just over-did it a bit. I'm putting her down for a rest."

"I can take her," Jeffery said, dropping the wood he'd brought. He brushed at his coat and pulled off his gloves as he crossed the clearing.

"Well, Lady Amhurst, it's twits or barbarians. Which do you prefer?" he questioned low enough that only Amelia could hear.

Amelia felt her breath quicken at the look Logan gave her. *What is happening to me? I'm acting like a schoolgirl. This must stop,* she thought and determined to feel nothing but polite gratitude toward Mr. Logan Reed. When she looked at each man and said nothing, Logan deposited her in Jeffery's waiting arms.

"Guess your feelings are pretty clear," he said and turned to leave.

"But I didn't say a thing, Mr. Reed," Amelia said, unconcerned with Jeffery's questioning look.

Logan turned. "Oh, but you did." As he walked away he called back to Jeffery, "Put her in her tent and help her with her bedroll. I'll have some food brought to her when it's ready."

"He's an extremely rude man, what?"

Amelia watched Logan walk away. She felt in some way she had insulted him, but surely he hadn't really expected her to choose him over Jeffery. He was only a simple American guide and Jeffery, well, Jeffery was much more than that. If only he were much more of something Amelia could find appealing.

"Put me down, Jeffery. I am very capable of walking and this familiarity is making me most uncomfortable," she demanded and Jeffery quickly complied. She knew deep in her heart that Logan would never be bullied in such a way.

"Mr. Reed said to have you lie down."

"I heard him and I'm quite capable of taking care of myself. Now shouldn't you help get the firewood? Mr. Reed also said we were to expect a cold night." Jeffery nodded and Amelia took herself to the tent, stopping only long enough to give Logan a defiant look before throwing back the flaps and secluding herself within.

"Men, like religion, are a nuisance," she muttered as she untied the strings on her bedroll.

six

Morning came with bone-numbing cold and Amelia was instantly grateful for her sisters. Snuggling closer to Penelope, Amelia warmed and drifted back to sleep. It seemed only moments later when someone was shouting her into consciousness and a loud clanging refused to allow her to ease back into her dreams.

"Breakfast in ten minutes!" Logan was shouting. "Roll up your gear and have it ready to go before you eat. Chamberlain, you will assist in taking down the tents."

Amelia rolled over and moaned at the soreness in her legs and backside. *Surely we aren't going to ride as hard today as yesterday.* Pushing back her covers, Amelia began to shiver from the cold of the mountain morning. *Could it have only been yesterday that the heat seemed so unbearable?* Stretching, Amelia decided that nothing could be worse than the days she'd spent on the Colorado prairie. *At least here, the black flies seem to have thinned out. Maybe the higher altitude and cold keeps them at bay.* Amelia squared her shoulders. *Maybe things are getting better.*

But it proved to be much worse. A half-day into the ride, Amelia was fervently wishing she could be swallowed up in one of the craggy ravines that threatened to eat away the narrow path on which she rode. The horse was cantankerous, her sisters were impossible, and Mattersley looked as though he might succumb to exhaustion before they paused for the night.

When a rock slide prevented them from taking the route Logan had planned on, he reminded the party again of the altitude and the necessity of taking it easy. "We could spend the next day or two trying to clear that path or we can spend an extra day or two on an alternate road into Estes. Since none of you are used to the thinner air, I think taking the other road makes more sense."

Logan's announcement made Amelia instantly self-conscious. *Was he making fun of me because of the attack I suffered last night? Why else would he make such an exaggerated point of the altitude?*

"I do hope the other road is easier," Lady Gambett said with a questioning glance at her husband.

"I'm afraid not," Logan replied. "It climbs higher, in fact, than this one and isn't traveled nearly as often. For all I know that trail could be in just as bad of shape as this one."

"Oh dear," Lady Gambett moaned.

"But Mama," Josephine protested, pushing her small spectacles up on the bridge of her nose, "I cannot possibly breathe air any thinner than this. I will simply perish."

Logan suppressed a snort of laughter and Amelia caught his eye in the process. His expression seemed to say "See, I told you so" and Amelia couldn't bear it. She turned quickly to Lady Gambett.

"Perhaps Josephine would be better off back in Longmont," Amelia suggested.

"Oh, gracious, perhaps we all would be," Lady Gambett replied.

"But I want to go on, Mama," the plumper Henrietta whined. "I'm having a capital time of it."

"We're all going ahead." Lord Gambett spoke firmly with a tone that told his women that he would brook no more nonsense.

"Are we settled and agreed then?" Logan asked from atop his horse.

"We are, sir." Gambett replied with a harsh look of reprimand in Josephine's direction.

Amelia tried to fade into the scenery behind Margaret's robust, but lethargic, palomino. The last thing in the world she wanted to do was to have to face Logan. She was determined to avoid him at any cost. Something inside her seemed to come apart whenever he was near. It would never do to have him believing her incapable of handling her emotions and to respond with anything but cool reservation would surely give him the wrong idea.

Logan was pushing them forward again. He was a harsh taskmaster and no one dared to question his choices—except for the times when Jeffery would occasionally put in a doubtful appraisal. Logan usually quieted him with a scowl or a raised eyebrow and always it caught Amelia's attention.

But she didn't want Logan Reed to capture her attention. She tried to focus on the beauty around her. Ragged rock walls surrounded them on one side, while what seemed to be the entire world, spread out in glorious splendor on the other side. The sheer drop made Amelia a bit light-headed, but the richness of the countryside was well worth the risk of traveling the narrow granite ledge. Tall pines were still in abundance, as were the quaint mountain flowers and vegetation Amelia had come to appreciate. Whenever they stopped to rest the horses she would gather a sample of each new flower and press it into her book, remembering in the back of her mind that Logan Reed would probably be the one to identify it later.

Soon enough the path widened a bit and Amelia kept close to Lady Gambett, hoping that both Jeffery and Logan would keep their distance. Her father was drawn into conversation with Lord Gambett, and Lady Gambett seemed more than happy for Amelia's company.

"The roses shouldn't be planted too deep, however," Lady Gambett was saying, and Amelia suddenly realized she hadn't a clue what the woman was talking about. "Now the roses at Havershire are some of the most beautiful in the world, but of course there are fourteen gardeners who devote themselves only to the roses."

Amelia nodded sedately and Lady Gambett continued rambling on about the possibility of creating a blue rose. Amelia's mind wandered to the rugged Logan Reed and when he allowed his horse to fall back a bit, she feared he might try to start up a conversation. Feeling her stomach do a flip and her breathing quicken, Amelia gripped the reins tighter and refused to look up.

"Are you ill, my dear?" Lady Gambett asked suddenly.

Amelia was startled by the question, but even more startled by the fact that Logan was looking right at her as if awaiting her answer. "I. . .uh. . .I'm just a bit tired." *It wasn't a lie,* she reasoned.

"Oh, I quite agree. Mr. Reed, shouldn't we have a bit of respite?" Lady Gambett inquired. "Poor Mattersley looks to be about to fall off his mount all together."

Logan nodded and held up his hand. "We'll stop here for a spell. See to your horses first."

Amelia tried not to smile at the thought of dismounting and stretching her weary limbs. She didn't want to give Logan a false impression and have him believe her pleasure was in him rather than his actions. Without regard to the rest of the party, Amelia urged her horse to a scraggly patch of grass and slid down without assistance. Her feet nearly buckled beneath her when her boots hit the ground. Her legs were so sore and stiff and her backside sorely abused. Rubbing the small of her back, she jumped in fear when Logan whispered her name.

"I didn't mean to scare you," he apologized. "I hope you're feeling better."

Amelia's mind raced with thoughts. She wanted desperately to keep the conversation light-hearted. "I'm quite well, thank you. Although I might say I've found a new way to extract a pound of flesh."

Logan laughed. "Ah, the dilemma of exacting a pound of flesh without spilling a drop of blood. The Merchant of Venice, right? I've read it several times and very much enjoyed it."

Amelia tried not to sound surprised. "You are familiar with Shakespeare?"

He put one hand to his chest and the other into the air. " 'My only love sprung from my only hate! Too early seen unknown, and known too late!' " He grinned. " 'Romeo and Juliet.' "

"Yes, I know," she replied, still amazed at this new revelation.

" 'Hatred stirreth up strifes: but love covereth all sins.' "

Amelia tried to remember what play these words were from, but nothing came to mind. "I suppose I don't know Shakespeare quite as well as you do, Mr. Reed."

"Logan," he said softly and smiled. "And it isn't Shakespeare's works, it's the Bible. Proverbs ten, twelve to be exact."

"Oh," she said and turned to give the horse her full attention.

"I thought we'd worked out a bit of a truce between us," Logan said, refusing to leave her to herself.

"There is no need for anything to be between us," Amelia said, trying hard to keep her voice steady. *How could this one man affect my entire being? She couldn't understand the surge of emotions, nor was she sure she wanted to.*

"It's a little late to take that stand, isn't it?" Logan asked in a whisper.

Amelia reeled on her heel as though the words had been hot coals placed upon her head. "I'm sure I don't understand your meaning, Mr. Reed," she said emphasizing his name.

"Now if you'll excuse me, I have other matters to consider."

"Like planting English roses?" he teased.

Her mouth dropped open only slightly before she composed her expression. "Have we lent ourselves to that most repulsive habit of eavesdropping, Mr. Reed?"

Logan laughed. "Who could help but overhear Lady Gambett and her suggestions? It hardly seemed possible to not hear the woman."

Amelia tried to suppress her smile, but couldn't. *Oh, but this man made her blood run hot and cold. Hot and cold.* She remembered Logan stating just that analysis of her back in Greeley. Just when she was determined to be unaffected by him, he would say or do something that made the goal impossible. She started to reply when Lady Gambett began to raise her voice in whining reprimand to Henrietta.

"It would seem," Amelia said, slowly allowing her gaze to meet his, "the woman speaks for herself."

Logan chuckled. "At every possible opportunity."

Lady Gambett was soon joined by Josephine, as well as Margaret and Penelope, and Amelia could only shake her head. "I'm glad they have each other."

"But who do you have?" Logan asked Amelia quite unexpectedly.

"I beg your pardon?"

"You heard me. You don't seem to have a great deal of affection for your sisters or your father. Sir Jeffery hardly seems your kind, although I have noticed he gives you a great deal of attention. You seem the odd man out, so to speak."

Amelia brushed bits of dirt from her riding jacket and fortified her reserve. "I need no one, Mr. Reed."

"No one?"

His question caused a ripple to quake through her resolve. She glanced to where the other members of the party were engaged in various degrees of conversation as they saw to their tasks. How ill-fitted they seemed in her life. She was tired of pretense and noble games, and yet it was the very life she had secured herself within. Didn't she long to return to England and the quiet of her father's estate? Didn't she yearn for a cup of tea in fine English china? Somehow the Donneswick estates seemed a foggy memory.

"Why are you here, Amelia?"

She looked up, thought to reprimand him for using her name, then decided it wasn't so bad after all. She rather liked the way it sounded on his lips. "Why?" she finally questioned, not truly expecting and answer.

"I just wondered why you and your family decided to come to America."

"Oh," she said, frowning at the thought of her father and Sir Jeffery's plans. There was no way she wanted to explain this to Logan Reed. He had already perceived her life to be one of frivolity and ornamentation. She'd nearly killed herself trying to work at his side in order to prove otherwise, but if she told him the truth it would defeat everything she'd done thus far. "We'd not yet toured the country and Lady Bird, an acquaintance of the family who compiled a book about her travels here, suggested we come immediately to Estes."

"I remember Lady Bird," Logan said softly. "She was a most unpretentious woman. A lady in true regard."

Amelia felt the challenge in Logan's words, but let it go unanswered. Instead, she turned the conversation to his personal life. "You are different from most Americans, Mr. Reed. You appear to have some of the benefits of a proper upbringing. You appear educated and well-read and you have better manners than most. You can speak quite eloquently when you desire to do so, or just as easily slip into that lazy American style that one finds so evident here in the West."

Logan grinned and gave his horse a nudge. "And I thought she didn't notice me."

Amelia frowned. "How is it that you are this way?"

Logan shrugged. "I had folks who saw the importance of an education, but held absolutely no regard for snobbery and uppity society ways. I went to college back east and learned a great deal, but not just in books. I learned about people."

"Is that where you also took up religion?" she questioned.

"No, not at all. I learned about God and the Bible from my mother and father first, and then from our local preacher. The things they taught me made a great deal of sense. Certainly more sense than anything the world was offering. It kept me going in the right direction."

Amelia nodded politely, but in the back of her mind she couldn't help but wonder about his statement. Most of her life she had felt herself running towards something, but it was impossible to know what that something was. Her mother had tried to encourage her to believe in God, but Amelia thought it a mindless game. Religion required you to believe in things you couldn't see or prove. Her very logical mind found it difficult to see reason in this. *If God existed, couldn't He make Himself known without requiring people to give in to superstitious nonsense and outrageous stories of miraculous wonders? And if God existed, why did tragedy and injustice abound? Why did He not, instead, create a perfect world without pain or sorrow?*

"I've answered your questions, now how about answering some of mine?" Logan's voice broke through her thoughts.

"Such as?" Amelia dared to ask.

"Such as, why are you really here? I have a good idea that Lady Bird has very little to do with your traveling to America."

Amelia saw her sisters move to where Jeffery stood and smiled. "My father wanted me to come, so I did. It pleased him and little else seemed to offer the same appeal."

"Is he still mourning your mother's passing?"

"I suppose in a sense, although it's been six years. They were very much a love match, which was quite rare among their friends."

"Rare? Why is that?"

Amelia smiled tolerantly. "Marriages are most generally arranged to be advantageous to the families involved. My father married beneath his social standing." She said the words without really meaning to.

"If he married for love it shouldn't have mattered. Seems like he did well enough for himself anyway," Logan replied. He nodded in the direction of her father in conversation with Mattersley. "He is an earl, after all, and surely that holds esteem in your social circles."

"Yes, but the title dies with him. He has no sons and his estates, well—" she found herself unwilling to answer Logan's soft spoken questions. "His estates aren't very productive. My mother had a low social standing, but she brought a small fortune and land into the family which bolstered my father's position."

"So it *was* advantageous to both families, despite her lack of standing?"

"Yes, but you don't understand. It made my father somewhat of an outcast. He's quite determined that his daughters do not make the same mistake. It's taken him years to rebuild friendships and such. People still speak badly of him if the moment presents itself in an advantageous way. Were we to marry poorly it would reflect directly on him and no doubt add to his sufferings."

"But what if you fall in love with someone your father deems beneath you?" Logan asked moving in a step. "Say you fall in love with a barbarian instead of a twit?" His raised brow implied what his words failed to say.

Amelia felt her face grow hot. *He is really asking what would happen if I fell in love with him.* His face was close enough to reach out and touch and as always that pesky mustache drew her attention. *What if?* She had to distance herself. She had to get away from his piercing green eyes and probing questions. "It could never happen, Mr. Reed," she finally said, then added with a hard stare of her own, "Never."

seven

Estes Park was like nothing Amelia had ever seen. Completely surrounded by mountains, the valley looked as though someone had placed it there to hide it away from the world. Ponderosa pine, spruce, and aspen dotted the area and Lord Amhurst was delighted to find the shrub-styled junipers whose berries were especially popular with the grouse and pheasants. She knew her father was becoming eager for the hunt. She had seen him eyeing the fowl while Jeffery had been watching the larger game.

They made their way slowly through the crisp morning air, horses panting lightly and blowing puffs of warm air out to meet the cold. To Amelia it seemed that the valley wrapped itself around them as they descended. Birds of varying kind began their songs, and from time to time a deer or elk would cross their path, pausing to stare for a moment at the intruders before darting off into the thicket.

Gone was the oppressive prairie with its blasting winds, insufferable heat, and swarming insects. Gone were the dusty streets and spittoons. This place was a complete contrast to the prairie towns she'd seen. Even the air was different. The air here, though thinner, was also so very dry and Amelia marveled at the difference between it and that of her native land. Already her skin felt tough and coarse and she vowed to rub scented oils and lotions on herself every night until they departed. But departing was the furthest thing from her mind. What had started out as an unpleasant obligation to her, was now becoming rather appealing. She found herself increasingly drawn to this strange land, and to the man who had brought them here.

She silently studied Logan's back as he rode. He was telling them bits and pieces of information about the area, but her mind wouldn't focus on the words.

What if she did fall in love with a barbarian? What if she already had?

⁂

The lodge where they'd made arrangements to stay was a two story log building surrounded by smaller log cabins. Lord Amhurst had arranged to take three cabins for his party, while Lord and Lady Gambett had decided to stay in the lodge itself. Lady Gambett had declared it necessary to see properly to the delicate constitutions of her daughters. This thought made Amelia want to laugh, but she remained stoically silent. Delicate constitutions had no place here and it would provide only one more weapon for Logan Reed to use against them. She was bound and determined to show Logan that English women could be strong and capable without need of anyone's assistance. Amelia chose to forget that Lady Bird had already proven her case to Logan Reed two years ago.

"This place looks awful," Margaret was whining as Mattersley helped to bring in their bags.

Amelia looked around the crude cabin and for once she didn't feel at all repulsed by the simplicity. It was one room with two beds, a small table with a single oil lamp, and a washstand with a pitcher and bowl of chipped blue porcelain that at one time might have been considered pretty. A stone fireplace dominated one wall. Red gingham curtains hung in the single window and several rag rugs had been strategically placed in stepping stone fashion upon the thin plank floor.

"It's quite serviceable, Margaret," Amelia stated firmly, "so stop being such a ninny. Perhaps you'd like to sleep in a tent again."

"I think this place is hideous," Penelope chimed in before Margaret could reply. "Papa was cruel to bring us here, and all because of you."

This statement came just as Logan appeared with one of several trunks containing the girls' clothes. He eyed Amelia suspiciously and placed the trunk on the floor. "I think you'll find this cabin a sight warmer than the tent and the bed more comfortable than the ground," he said before walking back out the door.

Amelia turned on her sisters with a fury. "Keep our private affairs to yourselves. I won't have the entire countryside knowing our business. Mother raised you to be ladies of quality and refinement. Ladies of that nature do not spout off about the family's personal concerns."

Margaret and Penelope were taken aback for only a moment. It mattered little to them that Logan Reed had overheard their conversation. Amelia knew that to them he was hired help, no different than Mattersley. They were quite used to a house filled with servants who overheard their conversations on a daily basis and knew better than to speak of the matters, even amongst themselves. Logan Reed was quite a different sort, however, and Amelia knew he'd feel completely within his rights to inquire about their statement at the first possible moment.

"I suggest we unpack our things and see if we can get the wrinkles out of our gowns. I'm sure you will want a bath and the chance to be rid of these riding costumes," Amelia said, taking a sure route she knew her sisters would follow.

"Oh, I do so hope to sink into a tub of hot water," Penelope moaned. At seventeen she was used to spending her days changing from one gown to another, sometimes wearing as many as six in the same day. "I'm positively sick of this mountain skirt or whatever they call it."

"I rather enjoy the freedom they afford," Amelia said.

Satisfied with having distracted her sisters, she unfastened the latches on the trunk. "But I would find a bath quite favorable."

They spent the rest of the day securing their belongings and laying out their claims on the various parts of the room. By standing their trunks on end they managed to create a separate table for each of them and it was here they placed their brushes, combs and perfumes. Helping Penelope to string a rope on which they could hang their dresses, Amelia realized they'd brought entirely too many formal gowns and not nearly enough simple outfits. *Where had they thought they were traveling? It wasn't as if they'd have anyone to dress up for.*

Logan came to mind and Amelia immediately vanquished his image from her thoughts. She would not concern herself with looking nice for him. Her father expected her to look the lovely English rose for Sir Jeffery. That was why the clothes were packed as they were. Her desires were immaterial compared to her father's.

❧

"Amelia has twice as many gowns as we have," Penelope complained at dinner that evening.

Lord Amhurst gave her a look of reprimand, but it was Lady Gambett who spoke. "Your sister is the eldest, and by being the eldest, she is to have certain privileges afforded her. You mustn't complain about it for once she's married and keeping house for herself, you shall be the eldest."

This placated the petite blond, but Amelia felt her face grow hot. She was grateful that Logan was nowhere to be seen.

"I suggest we make an early evening of it," the earl said with an eye to his daughters. "There is to be an early morning hunt and I'm certain you won't want to lag behind."

Margaret and Penelope began conversing immediately

with Henrietta and Josephine about what they would wear and how they would arrange their hair. Amelia could only think on the fact that she would be forced to spend still another day in Logan Reed's company.

"Papa," she said without giving the matter another thought, "I'd like to rest and walk about the grounds. Please forgive me if I decline the hunt."

The earl nodded, appraising her for a moment then dismissing the matter when Lady Gambett spoke up. "I will stay behind as well. I can't possibly bear the idea of another ride."

With the matter settled, the party dispersed and went to their various beds. Amelia faded to sleep quickly, relishing the comfort of a bed and the warmth of their fire. In her dreams she kept company with a green-eyed Logan, and because it was only a dream, Amelia found herself enjoying every single moment.

❧

Logan was glad to be home. The valley offered him familiar comfort that he had never been able to replicate elsewhere. His cabin, located just up the mountain, wasn't all that far from the lodge where he'd deposited the earl and his traveling companions. But, it was far enough. It afforded him some much needed privacy and the peace of mind to consider the matters at hand.

Kicking off his boots, Logan built a hearty fire and glanced around at his home. Three rooms comprised the first floor. The bedroom at the back of the cabin was small but served its purpose. A kitchen with a cookstove and several crude cupboards extended into the dining area where a table and chairs stood beneath one window. This area, in turn, blended into the main room where the fireplace mantel was lined with small tin-type photos and books. A comfortable sofa, which Logan had made himself, invited company which seldom came, and two idle chairs stood as sentinels beside a crude book shelf. The tall shelf of books seemed out of place for the rustic cabin, but it was Logan's private library and he cherished it more than any of his other possessions. Whenever he went out from the valley to the towns nearby, he always brought back new books to add to his collection. This time he'd picked up an order in Greeley and had five new books with which to pass the time. Two were works by Jules Verne that promised to be quite entertaining. Of the remaining three, one was a study of science, one a collection of poetry, and the final book promised an exploration of Italy.

With a sigh, Logan dropped down onto the sofa and glanced upward. Shadows from the dancing fire made images against the darkened loft. The house was silent except for the occasional popping of the fire, and Logan found his mind wandering to the fair-haired Lady Amelia. He knew he'd lost his heart to her, and furthermore he was certain that she felt something for him. He wanted to chide himself for his love at first sight reaction to the delicate beauty, but there was no need. His heart wouldn't have heeded the warning or reprimand. Lost in his daydreams, Logan fell asleep on the sofa. He'd see her tomorrow before the party went out on the hunt, but how would he manage the rest of the day without her at his side?

*

Amelia hung back in her cabin until well after her family had left for the hunting expedition. She was determined to keep from facing Logan Reed and having to deal with his comments or suggestions. She couldn't understand why he bothered her so much. *It wasn't as if he has any say in my life. It wasn't as if he could change my life, so why give him the slightest consideration?*

Making her way to the lodge, Amelia guessed it to be nearly eight o'clock. She could smell the lingering scents of breakfast on the air and knew that Logan had been right about one thing. Mountain air gave you a decidedly larger appetite.

"Morning," a heavy set woman Amelia knew to be the owner's wife called out. "You must be Lady Amhurst. Jonas told me you were staying behind this morning." Amelia nodded and the woman continued. "I'm just making bread, but you're welcome to keep me company."

Amelia smiled. "I thought to tour around the woods nearby, but I'd be happy to sit with you for a time, Mrs. Lewis." She barely remembered her father saying the place was owned by a family named Lewis.

The woman wiped her floury hands on her apron and reached for a bowl. "Just call me Mary. Mrs. Lewis is far too formal for the likes of me and this place."

Amelia sensed a genuine openness to the woman. "You must call me Amelia," she said, surprising herself by the declaration. The mountain air and simplicity of the setting made her forget old formalities. "What is it that you are doing just now?" she asked, feeling suddenly very interested.

Mary looked at her in disbelief. "Don't tell me you've never seen bread made before?"

"Never," Amelia said with a laugh. "I'm afraid I've never ventured much into the kitchen at all."

"But who does the cooking for your family?"

"Oh, we've a bevy of servants who see to our needs. Father believes that young women of noble upbringing have no place in a kitchen."

Mary laughed. "I guess I'm far from noble in upbringing. I was practically birthed in the kitchen." She kneaded the dough and sprinkled in a handful of flour. "Would you like to learn how to make bread?"

Surprised by an unfamiliar desire to do just that, Amelia responded. "I'd love to."

Mary wiped her hands again and went to a drawer where

he pulled out another apron. "Put this on over your pretty dress so that it doesn't get all messy. And take off those gloves. It doesn't pay to wear Sunday best when you're working in the kitchen."

She turned back to the dough, while Amelia secured the apron over what she had considered one of her dowdier gowns. The peach and green print was far from being her Sunday best. Amelia tucked her white kid gloves into the pocket of the apron and rolled up her sleeves like Mary's.

"I'm ready," she said confidently, anxious to embark on this new project. Lady Bird had told her that only in experiencing things first hand could a person truly have a working knowledge of them. One might read books about crossing the ocean or riding an elephant, but until you actually participated in those activities, you were only touching the memories of another.

"Here you go," Mary said, putting a large hunk of dough in front of her. "Work it just like this." She pushed the palms of her hands deep into the mass. "Then pull it back like this." Amelia watched, catching the rhythm as Mary's massive hands worked the dough. "Now you do it." Mary tossed a bit of flour atop the bread dough and smiled.

Amelia grinned. "You make it look simple enough." But it was harder than it looked. Amelia felt the sticky dough ooze through her fingers and laughed out loud at the sensation. *Father would positively expire if he saw me like this.*

"That's it," Mary said from beside her own pile. "You can work out a great many problems while kneading bread."

"I can imagine why," Amelia replied. Already her thoughts of Logan were fading.

She worked through two more piles of dough with Mary's lively chatter keeping her company. When all of the dough had been prepared Mary showed her how to divide the mass into loaves. Placing the last of her dough into one of the pans, Amelia wiped a stray strand of hair from her face and smiled. It was satisfying work. Twenty-two loaves lay rising before her and some of them had been formed by her own hands.

"There are so many," she commented, noting some of the dough had been placed in pans before her arrival. Already they were rising high, while still others filled the lodge with a delicious scent as they baked.

"I've been collecting bread pans for most of my life. Working this lodge takes a heap of bread for the folks who stay, as well as those who help out. I alternate the loaves so that some are always baking or rising or getting kneaded down. Bread is pretty much alike the country over, so travelers take right to it when they won't eat another thing on the table. And, I sell a few loaves on the side. Menfolk around here don't always want to bake their own bread, so they come here to buy it from me." As if on cue the door opened and Logan Reed strode in.

Amelia stared at him in stunned silence, while Logan did much the same. A lazy smile spread itself under the bushy mustache, making Amelia instantly uncomfortable. "You don't mean to tell me that Lady Amhurst is taking lessons in bread baking?"

"She sure is," Mary said, before Amelia could protest the conversation. "Amelia here is a right quick learner."

"Amelia, eh?" Logan raised a questioning brow to keep company with his lopsided smile.

"Sure," Mary said, betraying a bit of German heritage in her voice. "She's a charming young woman, this one."

"That she is," he replied then turned his question on Amelia, "Why aren't you on the hunt?"

Amelia couldn't tell him that she'd purposefully avoided the hunt because of him. She tossed around several ideas and finally decided on the closest thing to the truth. "I

anted to tour about the grounds. I've had enough horse-
acking for a while."

"I see."

For a moment Amelia was certain he really did see. His
xpression told her that he knew very well she'd made her
ecision based on something entirely apart from the dis-
omfort of the old cavalry saddle.

"Why are you here? I thought you'd be off with the others."
.melia knew that if he had doubted the reason for her deci-
ion, she had just confirmed those doubts.

Mary looked rather puzzled. "He comes for bread. One of
hose menfolk I told you about." She nudged Amelia play-
ully. "He's needs a good wife to keep him company and
nake his bread for him."

"Mary's right. That's probably just what I need," Logan
aid with a knowing look at Amelia.

"If you'll excuse me Mary, I'm going to go clean up and
ake my walk. I appreciate your lessons this morning."
Amelia untied the apron and put it across the back of a
nearby chair, her kid gloves forgotten in the pocket.

"Come back tomorrow morning and we'll make cinnamon
olls," the heavyset woman said with a smile.

"Now there's something every good wife should know,"
Logan piped up. "Mary's cinnamon rolls are the best in the
country. Why, I'd walk from Denver to Estes to get a pan of
those."

"If time permits, I'd be happy to work with you," Amelia
said and then hurried from the room.

Images of Logan Reed followed her back to the cabin
where Amelia hurriedly grabbed her journal and pencil, as
well as a straw walking-out hat. Balancing the journal while
tying on the bonnet, Amelia quickened her pace and determined to put as much distance as possible between her and
the smug-faced Mr. Reed. *Why couldn't he have just taken*

her party on the hunt and left her to herself? Why did he have to show up and see her wearing an apron and acting like hired help? But she'd enjoyed her time with Mary, and she never once felt like hired help. Instead she felt. . .well, she felt useful, as though she'd actually accomplished something very important.

Making her way along a tiny path behind the cluster of cabins, Amelia tried to grasp those feelings of accomplishment and consider what they meant. Her life in England seemed trite when she thought of Mary's long hours of work. She was idle in comparison, but then again, she had been schooled in the graceful arts of being idle. She could, of course, stitch lovely tea towels and dresser scarves. She could paint fairly well and intended to sketch out some pastoral scenes from her hike and later redo them in watercolors. But none of these things were all that useful. Mary's work was relied upon by those around her. She baked their bread and kept them fed. She braided rugs and sewed clothes to ward off the mountain chill. She worked with the hides her husband brought back from the hunts. She knew all of this because Mary had told her so in their chatty conversation. *Mary's is not an idle life of appearances. Mary's life has purpose and meaning.*

Before she realized it, Amelia was halfway up the incline which butted against the Lewis property. She turned to look back down and drew her breath in at the view. The sun gave everything the appearance of having been freshly washed. The brilliance of the colors stood out boldly against the dark green background of the snow-capped, tree-covered mountains. The rushing river on the opposite side of the property shimmered and gurgled in glorious shades of violet and blue. But it was always the lighting which appealed her painter's eyes. The light here was unlike any she'd ever seen before. It was impossible to explain, but for a moment she felt compelled to try. She sat down abruptly and took up her journal.

"There is a quality to the light which cannot be explained. It is, I suppose, due to the high mountain altitude and the thinner quality of oxygen," she spoke aloud while writing. "The colors are more vivid, yet, if possible, they are also more subtle. The lighting highlights every detail, while creating the illusion of something draped in a translucent veil. I know this doesn't make sense, yet it is most certainly so." She paused and looked down upon the tiny village. She would very much like to paint this scene, but how in the world could she ever capture the light?

Beside her were several tiny white flowers bobbing up and down in the gentle breeze. She leaned over on her elbow, mindless of her gown and watched them for a moment. She considered the contrast of their whiteness against the green of their leaves and wondered at their name. Plucking one stem, she pressed it between the pages of her book, jotted a note of its location and got to her feet.

The higher she climbed, the rougher the path. Finally it became quite steep and altogether impassable. It was here she decided to turn away from the path and make her own way. The little incline to her left seemed most appealing even though it was strewn with rocks. The way to her right was much too threatening with its jagged boulders and sheer drops. Hiking up her skirt, with her journal tucked under her arm, Amelia faced the challenging mountainside with a determined spirit. She was feeling quite bold and was nearly to the top when the loose gravel gave way beneath her feet and sent her tumbling backward. Sliding on her backside and rolling the rest of the way, Amelia finally landed in a heap at the foot of the incline. Six feet away stood Logan Reed with an expression on his face that seemed to contort from amusement to concern and back to amusement.

Amelia's pride and backside were sorely bruised, but she'd not admit defeat to Logan. She straightened her hat and frowned. "Are you spying on me, Mr. Reed?" she asked indignantly from where she sat.

Logan laughed. "I'd say you could use some looking after given the scene I just witnessed. But, no, I didn't mean to spy. I live just over the ridge so when I saw you walking up this way, I thought I'd come and offer my services."

Amelia quickly got to her feet and brushed the gravel from her gown. Seeing her book on the ground she retrieved it and winced at the way it hurt her to bend down. "Your services for what?" she asked, hoping Logan hadn't seen her misery as well.

"To be your hiking guide," he replied coming forward. "It would sure save you on your wardrobe." He pointed to a long tear in the skirt of her gown. "Why in the world did you hike out here dressed like that?"

"I beg your pardon?"

"At least that riding skirt would have been a little more serviceable. You need to have sturdy clothes to hike these hills," he chided.

"I will hike in whatever is most comfortable to me, Mr. Reed."

"And you think corsets and muslin prints are most comfortable?"

Amelia huffed. "I don't think it is any of your concern. I'm quite capable of taking care of myself."

Logan rolled his eyes and laughed all the harder. "Yes, I can see that." He shook his head and turned to walk back to the lodge, leaving Amelia to nurse her wounded pride.

eight

Amelia spent the rest of the morning making notes in her journal and contemplating Logan Reed. As much as she tried to forget him, she couldn't help thinking of his offer to be her hiking guide. *Logan knows every flower and tree in the area. He would certainly be the most knowledgeable man around when it came to identifying the vegetation and landmarks. If I am going to put together a book on the area it seems sensible to utilize the knowledge of the most intelligent man.*

The book idea wasn't really new to her. She'd been considering it since speaking with Lady Bird long before departing for America. Lady Bird told Amelia she should do something memorable with her time abroad. *Writing a book and painting dainty watercolor flowers seems very reasonable. Falling in love with a barbaric, American guide does not.*

Closing her book with loud snap, Amelia got to her feet. "I'm not in love," she murmured to the empty room. "I will not fall in love with Logan Reed." But even as she said the words, a part of Amelia knew that it was too late for such a declaration.

❧

At noon, she made her way to the lodge house where the hunting party had returned to gather for a large midday meal. Amelia saw that the hunt was successful, but for the first time she wondered about the business of cleaning the kill and how the skins of the animals were to be used afterward. She'd never given such matters much thought in the past. There was always someone else to do the dirty work.

"I say, Amelia, you missed quite a hunt. Sir Jeffery bagged a buck first thing out."

Amelia glanced at Jeffery and then back to her father. "How nice." She pulled out a chair and found Jeffery quickly at her side to seat her.

"It was a clean and easy shot, nothing so very spectacular," he said in false humility. "I could name a dozen animals that present a greater challenge to hunt."

"Perhaps the greatest challenge comes in bagging a wife, what?" Lord Amhurst heartily laughed much to Amelia's embarrassment and the stunned expressions of the others.

"Indeed true love is the hardest thing on earth to secure," Lady Gambett said in a tone that suggested a long story was forthcoming. She was fresh from a day of napping and eager to be companionable.

"Papa had a good morning as well," Penelope declared quickly and Margaret joined in so fast that both girls were talking at once. This seemed to be a cue to Josephine and Henrietta who began a garbled rendition of the hunt for their mother's benefit.

Jeffery took a chair at Amelia's right and engaged her immediately in conversation. "I missed your company on the hunt. Do say you'll be present tomorrow."

"I'm afraid I didn't come to America to hunt. Not for animals of any kind," she stated, clearly hoping the implied meaning would not be lost on Jeffery. The sooner he understood her distaste for their proposed matrimony, the better.

"What will you do with your time?"

Amelia folded her hands in her lap. "I plan to write a book on the flowers and vegetation of Estes Park." The words came out at just the exact moment that her sisters and the Gambetts had chosen to take a collective breath. Her words seemed to echo in the silence for several moments. Stunned faces from all around the table looked up to make certain they had heard correctly.

"You plan to do what?" Margaret asked before anyone else could give voice to their thoughts.

"You heard me correctly," Amelia said, taking up a thick slice of the bread she'd helped to make that morning. "The flowers here are beautiful and quite extraordinary. Nothing like what we have at home. Lady Bird told me I should use my time abroad to do something meaningful and memorable. I believe a book of this nature would certainly fit that suggestion."

The earl nodded. "If Lady Bird believes it to be of value, then I heartily agree." With Mattersley nowhere in sight, he filled his plate with potatoes and laughed when they dribbled over the rim. "Waiting on yourself takes some practice." The dinner party chuckled politely and the mood seemed to lighten considerably.

As everyone seemed intent on eating, Amelia's declaration passed from importance and escaped further discussion. With a sigh of relief, Amelia helped herself to a thick slice of ham and a hearty portion of potatoes. Jeffery would think her a glutton, but let him. She was tired of worrying about what other people thought. She found it suddenly quite enjoyable to be a bit more barbaric herself. Almost guilty for her thoughts, Amelia's head snapped up and she searched the room for Logan. She knew he wouldn't be there, but for some reason her conscience forced her to prove it.

"So how will you get about the place?" the earl was suddenly asking and all eyes turned to Amelia.

"I beg your pardon, Papa?"

"How will you travel about to gather your flowers and such? Will you have a guide?"

Amelia felt the ham stick in her throat as she tried to swallow. She took a long drink of her tea before replying.

"Mr. Reed has offered to act as guide, but I told him it wasn't necessary."

"Nonsense," her father answered. "If you are to undertake this project, do it in a correct manner. There is a great deal to know about this area and you should have a guide, what?"

"I suppose you are fair in assuming that," Amelia replied. "But I hardly think Mr. Reed would be an appropriate teacher on flowers."

Mary Lewis had entered the room to deposit two large pies on the table. "Logan's an excellent teacher," she said, unmindful of her eavesdropping. "Logan led an expedition of government people out here just last summer. He's got a good education—a sight more than most of the folks around these parts, anyway."

Everyone stared at Mary for a moment as though stunned by her boldness. "It seems reasonable," the earl said, nodding to Mary as if to dismiss her, "that Mr. Reed should direct you in your studies. I'll speak to him this afternoon and make certain he is reasonably recompensed for his efforts. Perhaps this evening at dinner we can finalize the arrangements."

Amelia said nothing. In truth, she had already decided to speak to Logan about helping her. She knew herself to be a prideful woman and what had once seemed like an admirable quality, now made her feel even more of a snob. Lady Bird had lowered herself to even help harvest the crops of local residents. How could she resist the help of Logan Reed, and possibly hope to justify herself. But just as her feelings were starting to mellow towards the man, he ruined it by joining them.

"Looks like you did pretty good for yourself, Amhurst," Logan said, taking a seat at the table.

Mary Lewis entered bringing him a huge platter of food. "I saved this for you, Logan."

"Much thanks, Mary." He bowed his head for a moment, before digging into the steaming food.

Everyone at the table looked on in silent accusation at Logan Reed. Even Mattersley would not presume to take his meals at the same table with the more noble classes. Logan Reed seemed to have no inclination that he was doing anything out of line, but when he glanced up he immediately caught the meaning of their silence. Rather than give in to their misplaced sense of propriety, however, Logan just smiled and complimented Mary on the food as she poured him a hot cup of coffee.

"Will Jonas be taking you out again tomorrow?" Logan asked as if nothing was amiss.

Amelia saw her father exchange a glance with Lord Gambett before answering. "Yes, I suppose he will. I understand you have offered to assist my daughter in gathering information for her book. I would like to discuss the terms of your employment after we finish with the meal."

Logan shook his head. "I didn't offer to be employed. I suggested to Lady Amhurst that I act as hiking guide and she refused." He looked hard at Amelia, but there was a hint of amusement in his eyes and his mustache twitched in its usual betraying fashion.

"It seemed improper to accept your suggestion," Amelia said rather stiffly.

"Nonsense, child. The man is fully qualified to assist you," Lord Amhurst stated. "I'll make all the arrangements after dinner."

Amelia felt Logan's eyes on her and blushed from head to toe. The discomfort she felt was nothing compared to what she knew would come if she didn't leave immediately. Surprising her family, she got up rather quickly.

"I beg your forgiveness, but I must be excused." Without waiting for her father's approval, Amelia left the room.

Much to her frustration, Jeffery Chamberlain was upon her heels in a matter of seconds. "Are you ill, Amelia?" His voice oozed concern.

"I am quite well," she replied, keeping a steady pace to her walk. "I simply needed to take the air."

"I understand perfectly," he replied and took hold of her elbow as if to assist her.

Amelia jerked away and once they had rounded the front of the lodge, she turned to speak her mind. "Sir Jeffery, there are some issues we must have settled between us."

"I quite agree, but surely you wouldn't seek to speak of them here. Perhaps we can steal away to a quiet corner of the lodge," he suggested.

Amelia shook her head. "I am sure what I desire to speak of will not be in keeping with what you desire to speak of."

"But Amelia—"

"Please give me a moment," she interrupted. Amelia saw his expression of concern change to one of puzzlement. She almost felt sorry for him. Almost, but not quite.

"You must come to understand," she began, "that I have no desire to follow my father's wishes and marry you." She raised a hand to silence his protests. "Please hear me out. My father might find you a wonderful candidate for a son-in-law, but I will not marry a man I do not love. And, Sir Chamberlain, I do not now, nor will I ever, love you."

The man's expression suggested anger and hurt, and for a moment Amelia thought to soften the blow. "However, my sisters find you quite acceptable as a prospective husband, so I would encourage you to court one of them."

At this Jeffery seemed insulted and puffed out his chest with a jerk of his chin. "I have no intentions of marrying your sisters," he said firmly. "I have an agreement with your father to acquire your hand in matrimony."

"But you have no such agreement with me, Sir Jeffery."

"It matters little. The men in our country arrange such affairs, not addle-brained women."

"Addle-brained?" Amelia was barely holding her anger in check. "You think me addle-brained?"

"When you act irresponsibly such as you are now, then yes, I do," he replied.

"I see. And what part of my actions implies being addle-brained?" she questioned. "Is it that I see no sense in joining in a marriage of convenience to a man I cannot possibly hope to love?"

"It is addle-brained and whimsical to imagine that such things as love are of weighted importance in this arrangement. Your father is seeing to this arrangement as he would any other business proposition. He is benefiting the family name, the family holdings, and the family coffers. Only a selfish and greedy young woman would see it as otherwise."

"So now I am addle-brained, whimsical, selfish, and greedy," Amelia said with haughty air. "Why in the world would you seek such a wife, Sir Chamberlain?"

Jeffery seemed to wilt a bit under her scrutiny. "I didn't mean to imply you were truly those things. But the air that you take in regards to our union would suggest you have given little consideration to the needs of others."

"So now I am inconsiderate as well!" Amelia turned on her heel and headed in the direction of the cabin.

Jeffery hurried after her. "You must understand, Amelia, these things are done for the betterment of all concerned."

She turned at this, completely unable to control her anger. "Jeffery, these things are done in order to keep my father in control of my mother's fortune. There hasn't been any consideration given to my desires or needs, and therefore I find it impossible to believe it has anything to do with my welfare or betterment."

"I can give you a good life," Jeffery replied barely keeping his temper in check. "I have several estates to where we might spend out our days and you will bring your own estate into the arrangement as well. You've a fine piece of Scottish land, or so your father tells me."

"But I have no desire to spend out my days with you. Not on the properties you already own, nor the properties which I might bring into a marriage. Please understand, so that we might spend our days here in America as amicably as possible," she said with determined conviction, "I will not agree to marry you."

Jeffery's face contorted and to Amelia's surprise he spoke out in a manner close to rage. "You will do what you are told and it matters little what you agree to. Your father and I have important matters riding on this circumstance and that alone is what will gain consideration. You will marry me, Amelia, and furthermore," he paused with a suggestive leer on his face, "you will find it surprisingly enjoyable."

"I would sooner marry Logan Reed as to join myself in union to a boorish snob such as yourself." Silently she wished for something to throw at the smug-faced Jeffery, but instead she calmed herself and fixed him with a harsh glare. "I pray you understand, and understand well. I will never marry you and I will take whatever measures are necessary to ensure that I win out in this unpleasant situation."

She stormed off to her cabin, seething from the confrontation, but also a bit frightened by Jeffery's strange nature. She'd never seen him more out of character and it gave her cause to wonder. She knew there had always been a mischievous, almost devious side to his personality. The memory of hanging over the banister in fear of plunging to her death on the floor below affirmed Amelia's consideration. Jeffery had always leaned a bit on the cruel side of practical jokes and teasing play. Still, she couldn't imagine that he was all that dangerous. He wanted something very badly from her father and no doubt he could just as easily obtain it by marrying one of her sisters. After all, they adored him.

Reaching her cabin, Amelia reasoned away her fears. Her father's insistence that she marry Jeffery was in order to preserve the inheritance. Perhaps there was some other legal means by which Amelia could waive rights to her portion of the estate. It was worth questioning her father. If he saw the sincerity of her desire to remain single, even to the point of giving up what her mother had planned to be rightfully hers, Amelia knew she'd have no qualms about doing exactly that.

"I would sooner marry Logan Reed." The words suddenly came back to haunt her. At first she laughed at this prospect while unfastening the back buttons of her gown. *What would married life be like with the likes of Logan Reed?* She could see herself in a cold cabin, kneading bread and scrubbing clothes on a washboard. She didn't even know how to cook and the thought of Logan laboring to choke down a meal prepared with her own two hands, made Amelia laugh all the harder.

The gown slid down from her shoulders and fell in a heap on the floor. Absentmindedly Amelia ran her hands down her slender white arms. Laughter died in her throat as an image of Logan doing the same thing came to mind. She imagined staring deep into his green eyes and finding everything she'd ever searched for. Answers to all her questions would be revealed in his soul-searching gaze, including the truths of life which seemed to elude her. Shuddering in a sudden wake of emotion, Amelia quickly pulled on the mountain skirt.

"He means nothing to me," she murmured defensively. "Logan Reed means nothing to me."

❧

Having dismissed himself from the dinner table on the excuse of bringing in wood for Mary, Logan had overheard most of the exchange between Jeffery and Amelia. At first he thought he might need to intercede on Amelia's behalf when Jeffery seemed to get his nose a bit out of joint, but the declaration of Amelia preferring to marry Logan over Jeffery had stopped him in his tracks.

At first he was mildly amused. He admired the young woman's spirit of defense and her ability to put the uppity Englishman in his place. He imagined with great pleasure the shock to Sir Chamberlain's noble esteem when Amelia declared her thoughts on the matter of marriage. At least it gave him a better understanding of what was going on between the members of the party. He'd felt an underlying current of tension from the first time he'd met them, especially between the trio of Lord Amhurst, Jeffery, and Amelia. Now, it was clearly understood that the earl planned to see his daughter married to Jeffery, and it was even clearer that Amelia had no desire to comply with her father's wishes. *But why?* Logan wondered. *Why would it be so important for the earl to pass his daughter off to Chamberlain?*

"I would sooner marry Logan Reed." He remembered the words and felt a bit smug. He knew she'd intended it as an insult to Jeffery, but it didn't matter. For reasons beyond his understanding, Logan felt as though he'd come one step closer to making Amelia his lady.

nine

In spite of her father's desire to have Amelia seek out Logan's assistance as her hiking guide, Amelia chose instead to hike alone. She was often up before any of the others and usually found herself in the kitchen of the lodge, learning the various culinary skills that Mary performed.

"You're doing a fine job, Amelia," Mary told her.

Amelia stared down at the dough rings as they floated and sizzled in a pool of lard. "And you call these doughnuts?" she questioned, careful to turn them before they burned on one side.

"Sure. Sure. Some folks call them oly koeks. The menfolk love 'em though. I could fix six dozen of these a day and have them gone by noon. Once the men learn doughnuts are on the table, I can't get rid of them 'til they get rid of the doughnuts."

Amelia laughed. They didn't seem all that hard to make and she rather enjoyed the way they bobbed up and down in the fat. It reminded her of the life preservers on board the ship they'd used to cross the Atlantic. "I'll remember that."

"Sure, you'll make a lot of friends if you fix these for your folks back in England," Mary replied.

Amelia couldn't begin to imagine the reaction of her "folks back in England" should they see her bent over a stove, laboring to bring doughnuts to the table. "I'm afraid," she began, "that it would never be considered appropriate for me to do such a thing at home."

"No?" Mary seem surprised. "I betcha they'd get eaten."

"Yes, I'd imagine after everyone recovered from the fits of

apoplexy, they just might eat the doughnuts." She pulled the rings from the grease and sprinkled them with sugar just as Mary had shown her to do. It was while she was engrossed in this task that Logan popped his head through the open doorway.

"Ummm, I don't have to ask what you're doing today, Mary."

"Ain't me, Logan. It's Amelia. She's turning into right handy kitchen help."

Logan raised a brow of question in Amelia's direction. "I don't believe it. Let me taste one of those doughnuts." He reached out before Amelia could stop him and popped half of the ring into his mouth. His expression changed as though he were considering a very weighty question. Without breaking his stoic expression he finished the doughnut and reached for another. "I'd better try again." He ate this one in three bites instead of two and again the expression on his face remained rigidly set. "Mary, better pour me a cup of coffee. I'm going to have to try another one in order to figure out if they're as good as yours or maybe, just maybe, a tiny sight better."

Amelia flushed crimson and turned quickly to put more rings into the grease before Logan spoke again. "Now I know we'll have to keep this one around."

Mary laughed and brought him the coffee. "That's what I keep tellin' her. I don't know when I've enjoyed a summer visitor more. Most young ladies of her upbringin' are a bit more uppity. They never want to learn kitchen work, that's for sure."

Amelia tried not to feel pride in the statement. She knew full well that Logan had once considered her one of those more uppity types and rightly so. For the past few weeks even Amelia couldn't explain the change in her attitude and spirit. She found the countryside inspiring and provoking, and with each passing day she felt more and more a part of this land.

Not realizing it she shook her head. *I'm English,* she thought and turned the doughnuts. *I cannot possibly belong to this place.* She looked up feeling a sense of guilt and found Logan's gaze fixed on her. A surge of emotion raced through her. *I cannot possibly belong to this man.*

Swallowing hard, she took a nervous glance at her pocket watch. "Oh, my," she declared, brushing off imaginary bits of flour and crumbs, "I must go. I promised I'd wake Margaret by seven."

Mary nodded. "You go on now. I've had a good long rest."

"Hardly that," Amelia said and took off her apron. "I have been here three weeks and I have yet to see you rest at any time."

"I saw it once," Logan said conspiratorially, "but it was six years ago and Mary was down sick with a fever. She sat down for about ten minutes that day, but that was it."

Amelia smiled in spite of herself. "I thought so. Thanks for the lesson, Mary. I'll see you later." She hurried from the room with a smile still brightening her face.

"Don't forget," Mary reminded, "you wanted to start quilting and this afternoon will be just fine for me."

"All right. I should be free," she replied over her shoulder.

"Hey, wait up a minute," Logan called and joined her as she crossed from the lodge to the grassy cabin area.

Looking up, Amelia felt her pulse quicken. "What is it?"

"I was hoping you'd be interested in a hike with me. I thought you'd like to go on a real adventure."

Amelia's curiosity was piqued. "What did you have in mind?"

"Long's Peak."

"The mountain?"

Logan grinned. "The same. There's quite a challenging climb up to the top. If you think you're up to it, I could approach your father on the matter."

"He'd never agree to such a thing."

Logan's smile faded. "He wouldn't agree, or you don't agree?"

Amelia felt a twinge of defensiveness but ignored it. She found herself honestly wishing she could hike up Long's Peak with Logan Reed and to argue now wouldn't help her case one bit. "Without an appropriate chaperon, Logan," she said his name hoping to prove her willingness, "it would never be allowed."

Logan cheered at this. "So what does it take to have an appropriate chaperon?"

"Someone like Mary or Lady Gambett."

Logan nodded. "I guess I can understand that. I'll work on it and let you know."

Amelia saw him turn to go and found a feeling of deep dissatisfaction engulfing her. "Logan, wait."

He turned back and eyed her questioningly. "Yes?"

"I've collected quite a variety of vegetation and flower samples and I thought, well actually I hoped—" she paused seeing that she held his interest. "I was too hasty in rejecting your offer of help. My father wanted me to accept and so now I'm asking if you would assist me in identifying my samples."

"What made you change your mind?" he asked softly coming to stand only inches away. His eyes were dark and imploring and Amelia felt totally swallowed up in their depths.

"I'm not sure," Amelia said, feeling very small and very vulnerable.

Logan's lopsided grin made his entire face light up. "It doesn't matter. I'd be happy to help you. When do you want to start?"

"How would this morning work out for you? Say, after the others have gone about their business?"

"That sounds good to me. I'll meet you at the lodge."

Amelia smiled and gave a little nod. It had been a very agreeable conclusion to their conversation. She watched Logan go off in the direction of the lodge and thought her heart would burst from the happiness she felt. *What was it? Why did she suddenly feel so light?* For weeks she had fought against her nature and her better judgment regarding Logan Reed. Now, giving in and accepting Logan's help seemed to free rather than burden her.

She approached the cabin she'd been sharing with her sisters and grew wary at the sound of voices inside.

"Amelia is simply *awful*. She gives no consideration to family, or to poor Papa's social standing." It was Penelope, and Margaret quickly picked up the challenge.

"Amelia has never cared for anyone but Amelia. I think she's hateful and selfish. Just look at the gowns she has to choose from and you and I must suffer through with only five apiece. I'm quite beside myself."

"And all because Papa is trying to see her married to poor Jeffery. Why he doesn't even love Amelia, and she certainly doesn't love him. I overheard Papa tell him that he would give him not only a substantial dowry, but one of the Scottish estates, if only Jeffery could convince Amelia to marry him before we returned to England."

"She'll never agree to it," Margaret replied haughtily. "She doesn't care one whit what happens to the rest of us. She never bothers to consider what might make others happy. If she hurts Papa this way and ruins my season in London, I'll simply die."

Amelia listened to the bitter words of her sisters and felt more alone than she'd ever felt before. Her entire family saw her only as an obligation and a threat to their happiness. *Surely there is some way to convince them that I don't care about the money. All I really want is a chance to fall in love and settle down with the right man.* Instantly Logan Reed's image filled her mind and Amelia had to smile. She would truly scandalize her family if she suggested marriage to Mr. Reed.

The conversation inside the cabin once again drew her attention when Penelope's whining voice seemed to raise an octave in despair. "I hate her! I truly do. She's forced us to live as barbarians and traipse about this horrid country, and for what? So that she can scorn Sir Jeffery, a man in good standing with the queen herself?"

Amelia felt the bite of her sister's words. She'd never considered her siblings to be close and dear friends, but now it was apparent that even a pretense of affection was out of the question. Hot tears came unbidden to her eyes and suddenly years of pent up emotion would no longer be denied.

"Oh, Mama," she whispered, wiping desperately at her cheeks, "why did you leave me without love?" Gathering up her skirt, Amelia waited to hear no more. She ran for the coverage of the pines and aspens. She ran for the solitude of the mountainous haven which she'd grown to love.

Blinded by her own tears, Amelia fought her way through the underbrush of the landscape. She felt the biting sting of the branches as they slapped at her arms and face, but the pain they delivered was mild compared to the emptiness within her heart. Panting for air, Amelia collapsed beside a fallen spruce. Surrendering to her pain, she buried her face in her hands and sobbed long and hard.

It isn't fair. It wasn't right that she should have to bear such a thing alone. Her mother had been the only person to truly care about her and now she was forever beyond her reach. A thought came to Amelia. *Perhaps a spiritualist could put her in touch with her mother's spirit.* Then just as quickly as the thought came, Amelia banished it. In spite of the fact that spiritualists were all the rage in Europe and

America, she didn't believe in such things. *Life ended at the grave—didn't it?*

"I don't know what to believe in anymore," she muttered.

She was suddenly ashamed of herself and her life. She wasn't really a snob, as Logan had presumed her to be. Her upbringing had demanded certain things of her, however. She didn't have the same freedoms as women of lower classes. She wasn't allowed to frolic about and laugh in public. She wasn't allowed to speak her mind in mixed company, or to have her opinion considered with any real concern once it was spoken. Amelia found herself envying Mary and her simple, but hard life here in the Rocky Mountains. The men around Mary genuinely revered and cared for her. Her husband had no reason to fear when he took a party out hunting, because everyone looked out for Mary.

I wish I could be more like her, Amelia thought, tears pouring anew from her eyes. She'd not cried this much since her mother's passing. Mother was like Mary. Amelia could still see her mother working with her flowers in the garden wearing a large straw bonnet cocked to one side to shield her from the sun, and snug, mud-stained gloves kept her hands in ladylike fashion. Amelia traced the fingers of her own hands, realizing that she'd forgotten her gloves. *Oh, Mama, what am I to do?*

Looking up, Amelia was startled to find Logan sitting on a log not ten feet away. "What are you doing here?" she asked, dabbing at her eyes with the edge of her skirt.

"I saw you run up here and got worried that something was wrong. Generally, folks around here don't run like their house is on fire—unless it is." He gave her only a hint of a smile.

Amelia offered him no explanation. It was too humiliating even to remember her sister's words, much less bring them into being again by relating them to Logan.

Seeming to sense her distress, Logan leaned back and put

his hands behind his head. He looked for all the world as though he'd simply come out for a quiet moment in the woods. "There's an old Ute Indian saying that starts out, 'I go to the mountain where I take myself to heal, the earthly wounds that people give to me.' I guess you aren't the first person to come seeking solace, eh?"

"I'm not seeking anything," Amelia replied, feeling very vulnerable knowing that Logan had easily pegged her emotions.

"We're all seeking something, Amelia," Logan said without a hint of reprimand. "We're all looking to find things to put inside to fill up the empty places. Some people look for it in a place, others in things, some in people." His eyes pierced her soul and Amelia looked away as he continued. "Funny thing is, there's only so much you can fill up with earthly things. There's an empty place and a void inside that only God can fill and some folks never figure that out."

"You forget, Mr. Reed," she said in protected haughtiness, "I don't believe in the existence of God." The words sounded hollow even to Amelia.

Logan shrugged. "You're sitting in the middle of all this beauty and you still question the existence of God?"

"I've been among many wonders of the world, Mr. Reed. I've traveled the Alps, as well as your Rockies, and found them to be extraordinarily beautiful as well. What I did not find, was God. I find no proof of an almighty being in the wonders of the earth. They are simple, scientifically explained circumstances. They are nothing more than the visual representation of the geological forces at work in this universe. It certainly doesn't prove the existence of God." She paused to look at him quite seriously. "If it did, then I would have to counter with a question of my own."

"Such as?"

"Such as, if the beauty of the earth proclaims the existence of God, then why doesn't the savagery and horrors of the world do as much to denounce His existence? This God you are so fond of quoting and believing in must not amount to much if He stands idly by to watch the suffering of His supposed creation. I've seen the beauty of the world, Mr. Reed, but so too, have I seen many of its tragedies and injustices. I've been in places where mothers murder their children rather than watch them starve to death slowly. I've seen old people put to death because they are no longer useful to their culture. I've beheld squalor and waste just as surely as I've seen tranquility and loveliness, and none of it rises up to assure me of God's existence."

"Granted, there's a lot wrong in this world, but what about the forces of evil? Don't you think evil can work against good and interfere with God's perfect plan? When people stray from the truth, the devil has the perfect opportunity to step in and stir up all kinds of chaos."

"Then your God isn't very strong, is He?" She lifted her chin a little higher. "As I recall, the devil you believe exists is a fallen angel named Lucifer. Is not your God more powerful than a fallen angel? Don't you see, Mr. Reed, these are nothing more than stories designed to make mankind feel better about itself and the world. The poor man trudges through life believing that even though he has nothing on earth, he will have a celestial mansion when he dies. A rather convenient way of bolstering spirits and keeping one's nose to the grindstone, don't you think?"

Logan shook his head. "You're talking about something you obviously know very little about. An eternal home in heaven isn't all that the repentant sinner has to look forward to."

"No?" She looked away as though studying the trees around them. "I suppose you will tell me that he can pray and have his desires magically met by a benevolent God who wants His children to live in abundance and earthly wealth."

"Not at all. God isn't in charge of some heavenly mercantile where you step in and order up whatever your little heart wants. No, Amelia, I'm talking about living in truth. Knowing that you are following the path God would have you travel, and in knowing that, you will find the satisfaction of truth, faithfulness, peace, and love."

"Oh, please," Amelia said meeting his eyes. "This is all religious rhetoric and you know it. The fact of the matter is that truth is completely in the heart and mind of the person or persons involved. I see the truth as one thing and you obviously see it as another. Do not believe I'm any less satisfied for the things I believe in, because I assure you I am not." She bit her lip and looked away. She could hardly bear to meet his expression, knowing that deep inside, the things she believed in were not the least bit satisfying.

As if reading her mind, Logan sat up and said, "I feel sorry for you Amelia. You are afraid to consider the possibility that there is a God, because considering it might force you to reckon with yourself."

"I don't know what you mean." She got to her feet and brushed off the dirt and leaves that clung to her skirt.

Logan jumped to his feet. "That's it. It's really a matter of you being afraid."

Amelia bit at her lower lip again and looked at the ground. "I need to get back. They'll have missed me at breakfast."

Logan crossed the distance to stop her. Putting his hand out, he took hold of her arm and gently turned her back to face him. "God can fill that void inside, Amelia. He can wrap you in comfort and ease your burden. He can be all that human folks fail to be."

Amelia pushed him away. She was, for the first time in a long, long time, frightened. Not of Logan Reed, but of what he represented. "I have to go."

"In a minute," Logan said softly. "First tell me why you were crying."

Amelia shook her head. "It was nothing. Nothing of importance."

Logan reached out and before Amelia could move, he smoothed back a bit of hair from her face and stroked her cheek with his fingers. "It's important to me." His voice was barely a whisper.

Amelia stared up at him and found herself washed in the flood of compassion that seemed to emanate from his eyes. Her mouth went dry and her heart pounded so hard that she was sure Logan could hear it. She struggled with her emotions for a full minute before steadying her nerves to reply. "I don't want to be important to you."

Logan laughed. "Too late. You already are."

Amelia balled her hands into fists and struck them against her side. "Just leave me alone, Logan. I can't do this."

Logan looked at her in surprise. "Do what?"

Amelia opened her mouth as if to speak, then quickly shut it again. She had nearly said, "Love you." Now, standing here in the crisp freshness of morning, Amelia knew beyond doubt, that Logan understood exactly what she'd nearly said. "I can't do this," was all she could say.

Logan backed away. "I have an idea. Why don't you come on a hike with me tomorrow? Your family and friends will be on an overnight hunt, I heard Jonas telling Mary all about it after you left the kitchen. We could spend the whole day gathering your samples and I could spend all evening telling you what they are."

"I don't think—"

"Don't think," Logan said with such longing in his voice that Amelia couldn't ignore his plea.

"All right," she said quickly, hoping that if she agreed to his suggestion he'd leave her alone. There'd be plenty of time to back out of the invitation later. Later, when she was calmer and could think more clearly. Later when the warmth of Logan's green eyes didn't melt the icy wall she'd built between them.

Logan's mustache twitched as it always did before his lips broke into a full smile. "I'm holding you to it."

Amelia nodded and started back down the mountain. Two things deeply troubled her. One was Logan's words about God. The other was Logan, himself.

ten

Logan had spent a restless day and night thinking of what his hike with Amelia might accomplish. He saw the desperation in her eyes. He knew she longed to understand what was missing in her life. But how could he lead her to the truth about God, when she didn't believe in the validity of God? Usually, whenever he witnessed to someone, Logan knew he could rely on the Scriptures to give them something solid that they could put their hands on—the written word of God. That seemed to be important to folks. With Amelia's disbelief in God and her position that the Bible was nothing more than the collective works of men from the past, Logan felt at a loss as to how he could proceed without it. His mother and other Christians he'd known had assured him that all he needed was a faith in God and in His word. And even now, Logan believed that was still true. But what he couldn't figure out was how to apply it all and show Amelia the way to God. Somehow, he felt, he must be failing as a Christian if this simple mission eluded him. *How can I defend my faith in God and show Amelia the truth, when it is that very truth that makes her run in the opposite direction?*

Logan took up his Bible and sat down to a self-prepared breakfast of smoked ham and scrambled eggs. He opened the book and bowed his head in prayer. "Father, there's a great deal of hurt inside Amelia Amhurst. I know You already see her and love her. I know You understand how to reach her. But I don't know how to help and I seek Your guidance and direction. I want to help her find her way home to You. Give me the right words and open her heart to

Your Spirit's calling. In Jesus' name I pray, Amen."

Logan opened his eyes and found comfort in the Scripture before him. "The Spirit itself beareth witness with our spirit, that we are the children of God," he read aloud from the eighth chapter of Romans. A peace came over him and he smiled. God's Spirit would speak for him. It wasn't Logan Reed's inspirational words or evidence that would save Amelia, it was God's Holy Spirit. The Holy Spirit would also show her the validity of the Bible. He needn't compromise his beliefs and put the Bible aside. Neither did he need to go out of his way to defend God. God could fully take care of all the details.

He almost laughed out loud at the way he'd taken it all on his own shoulders. It was typical of him to rush in and try to arrange things on his own. But now, he didn't have to and God had made that quite clear. Amelia Amhurst was here for a reason. Not for her father's matrimonial desires or Chamberlain's financial benefits in joining with her. Amelia was here because God knew it was time for her to come to the truth. The Holy Spirit would bear witness to Amelia that not only was God real, but that she had a way to reconcile herself with Him. With a lighter heart, Logan dug into his breakfast and prepared for the day.

❧

Logan whistled a tune as he came into the lodge through the kitchen. He found Amelia bent over a sink-full of dishes and paused to consider her there. Her blond hair was braided in a simple fashion to hang down her back and the clothes she wore were more austere than usual. She no longer appeared the refined English rose, but rather looked to be the descendant of hearty pioneer stock.

"I see you dressed appropriately," he said from behind her.

Amelia whirled around with soapy hands raised as though Logan had threatened a robbery. In a rather breathless voice she addressed him. "I borrowed some clothes from Mary." Gone was any trace of her agitation with him the day before.

"Good thinking." Logan felt unable to tear his gaze away from her wide blue eyes.

"She gave me some sturdy boots, as well." Amelia's voice was a nervous whisper as soap suds dripped down her arms and puddled onto the wood floor.

"You gonna be much longer with those?" Logan asked, nodding toward the sink, but still refusing to release her gaze.

"No. I'm nearly finished."

"I can help," he offered.

"No. Why don't you have a cup of coffee instead? I can see to this."

Amelia was the one who finally turned away. Logan thought her cheeks looked particularly flushed, but he gave the cookstove and fireplace credit for this and took a cup. Pouring rich, black coffee, Logan nearly burned himself as his glances traveled back and forth between Amelia and the coffee.

"How'd the quilting lesson go yesterday?" he asked.

"My stitches were as big as horses," Amelia admitted, "but Mary told me not to worry about it. She said it was better to work at consistency and spacing."

"Mary should know. She does beautiful work."

"Yes, she does." Amelia finished with her task and dried her hands on her apron. "I don't suppose I'll ever do such nice work."

"You don't give yourself enough credit. Look how quick you took to making doughnuts. When you reach Mary's age you'll be every bit as good at making quilts as she is. "

"I seriously doubt that," she replied and Logan thought she sounded rather sad. "You see, once we return to England, I know it will hardly be acceptable for me to sit about making quilts and frying doughnuts."

"Maybe you shouldn't go back."

The words fell between them as if a boulder had dropped into the room. Sensing Amelia's inability to speak on the matter, Logan changed the subject. "Well, I have a knapsack full of food, so if you're ready—"

Amelia nodded and untied her apron. "Let me get my coat." She hurried over to a nearby chair and pulled on a serviceable broadcloth coat. The jacket was several sizes too big, obviously another loan from Mary, but Logan thought she looked just right.

Smiling he nodded. "You look perfect."

"Hardly that, Mr. Reed, but I am. . .well—" she glanced down at her mismatched attire and raised her face with a grin, "I am prepared."

He laughed. "Well, out here that suggests perfection. A person ought to always be prepared. You never know when a storm will blow up or an early snow will keep you held up in your house. Preparation is everything."

❧

The sun was high overhead before Logan suggested they break for lunch. Amelia was secretly relieved and plopped down on the ground in a most unladylike manner. The scenery around her was hard to ignore. The rocky granite walls were imposing and gave her a powerful reminder of how little she knew of taking care of herself. *What if something happened to Logan? How would I ever return to Estes without his assistance?*

"You up to one more thing before I break out the chow?"

Amelia looked up and hoped that the weariness she felt was hidden from her expression. "I suppose so." She made a motion to get up, but before she could move Logan reached down and lifted her easily.

"You look pretty robust," he said, dropping his hold, "but

you weigh next to nothing. I've had dogs that weighed more than you."

Amelia thought it was a strange sort of observation, but then remembered back in Greeley when her beauty had been compared to a polished spittoon. "And I've had horses more mannerly than you," she finally replied, "but I don't hold that against you and I pray you won't hold my weight against me."

"You pray?" he said, acting surprised.

"It's a mere expression, I assure you. Now please show me what you had in mind and then feed me before I perish."

Logan took hold of her hand and pulled her along as though they traveled in this manner all of the time. He walked only a matter of ten or twelve steps, however, before drawing Amelia up to a frightening precipice.

"Oh, my!" she gasped gazing over the edge of the sheer drop. She clung to Logan's hand without giving thought to what he might think. "How beautiful," she finally added, gazing out beyond the chasm. A tiny ledge of rock stuck out some six or seven feet below them, but after that there was nothing but the seemingly endless open spaces below. Beyond them, the Rocky Mountain panorama stretched out and Amelia actually felt a lump form in her throat. There were no words for what she was feeling. Such a rush of emotions simply had no words. It was almost as if this country beckoned to her inner soul. She felt something here that she'd never known anywhere else. Not in the Alps with all of their grandeur. Not amongst the spicy, exotic streets of Egypt. Not even on her father's estate in England.

Her eyes scanned the scene and her mind raced with one pounding sensation. When her eyes settled on Logan's face, that sensation was realized in a single word. *Home. I feel,* she thought, *as though I've come home.*

For a moment she thought Logan might kiss her, and for

as long a moment, she wished he would. She longed for his embrace. The warmth of his hand on hers drew her further away from thoughts of her family and England. *Is this true love? Are this man and this place to forever be a part of my destiny? Yet how could it be? How could I even imagine it possible?* She was a refined English lady—the daughter of an earl. She had been presented to Queen Victoria and had even made the acquaintances of the princesses.

Logan's voice interrupted the awe-inspired moment. "Come on, let's eat."

He pulled her back to the place where she'd rested earlier, and without ceremony, plopped himself down on the ground and began wrestling with the knapsack. Amelia was very nearly devastated. *Didn't he feel it too? Didn't he feel the compelling, overwhelming attraction to her that she felt to him?*

Chiding herself for such unthinkable emotions, Amelia sat down and took the canteen Logan offered her. She drank slowly, the icy liquid quenching her thirst, but not her desire to know more. *But what is it that I want to know?* She refused to be absorbed with questions of immortality and religious nonsense, and yet there were so many questions already coming to mind.

Logan slapped a piece of ham between two thick slices of Mary's bread and handed the sandwich over to Amelia. "It's not fancy, but I promise you it will taste like the finest banquet food you've ever had."

Amelia nodded and nibbled on the edge of the crust. She was famished and yet, when Logan bowed his head in prayer, she paused in respectful silence, not really knowing why. When he finished, he pulled out a napkin and revealed two pieces of applesauce cake.

"Mary had these left over from last night and I thought they'd make a great dessert."

"Indeed they would," Amelia agreed and continued eating the sandwich.

In between bites of his own food, Logan began sharing a story about the area. "This is called Crying Rock," he explained.

"Why Crying Rock?" Amelia asked, looking around her to see if some rock formation looked like eyes with water flowing from it.

"Legend holds that an Indian warrior fell to his death from that very spot where we stood just minutes ago. He had come to settle a dispute with another warrior and in the course of the fight, he lost his life."

"How tragic. What were they fighting about?" Amelia asked, genuinely interested.

"A young woman," he said with a grin. "What else?"

Amelia jutted out her chin feeling rather defensive. "How foolish of them both."

"Not at all. You see the warrior was in love with a woman who was already pledged to marry the other man. It was arranged by her father, but her heart wasn't in it. She was in love with the other warrior."

Amelia felt the intensity of his stare and knew that he understood her plight in full. She felt more vulnerable in that moment than she'd ever felt in her life. It was almost as if her entire heart was laid bare before Logan Reed. She wished she could rise up with dignity and walk back to the lodge, but she hadn't the remotest idea how she could accomplish such a feat. Instead, she finished her sandwich and drank from the canteen before saying, "Obviously, she lost out in this situation and had to marry the man she didn't love."

Logan shook his head. "Not exactly. After the death of her true love, she was to marry the victor in five days and so she brought herself up here and sat down to a period of mourning. As legend tells it, she cried for four straight days. The people could hear her, clear down in the village below and folks around here say at night when the wind blows it can still sound just like a woman crying."

"What happened after that?" Amelia asked, almost against her will.

"On the fifth day she stopped crying. She washed, dressed in her wedding clothes and offered up a final prayer in honor of her lost warrior," Logan paused and it seemed to Amelia that he'd just as soon not continue with the story.

"And?" she pressed.

"And, she threw herself off the rock and took her own life."

"Oh." It was all Amelia could say. She let her gaze go to the edge of the rock and thought of the devastated young woman who died. She could understand the woman's misery. Facing a life with Jeffery Chamberlain was akin to a type of death in and of itself. And then, for the first time, the realization that she would most likely be forced to marry Jeffery, truly sunk in. The tightness in her chest made her feel suddenly hemmed in. Her father would never allow her to walk out of this arrangement. There was no way he would care for her concerns or her desires to marry for love. The matter was already settled and it would hardly be affected by Amelia's stubborn refusal.

"You okay?" Logan asked softly.

She looked back to him and realized that he'd been watching her the whole time. "I'm, well—" she fell silent and tried to reorganize her thoughts. "The story was fascinating and I was just thinking that perhaps a book on Indian lore would be more beneficial than one on wild flowers."

Logan seemed to consider this a moment. "Why not combine them. You could have your flowers and identification information and weave in stories of the area. After all, the summer is coming quickly to an end and you've already done a great deal of work on the area vegetation."

"Would you teach me more about the lore from this area?" she asked, swallowing down the depression that threatened to engulf her.

"Sure," he said, so nonchalant that Amelia knew he didn't understand her dilemma.

No one understands, she thought as a heavy sigh escaped her lips. *No one would ever understand.*

eleven

A week and a half later, Amelia watched as Mary finished packing a saddlebag with food. "Mary, are you sure that you and Jonas want to do this?" she questioned quite seriously. "I mean, Long's Peak looks to be a very serious climb."

"Oh, it's serious enough," she said with a smile. "I've made it four times before, I figure number five ain't gonna kill me."

"You've climbed up Long's Peak four times?" Amelia questioned in disbelief.

Logan laughed at her doubtful expression. "Mary's a great old gal and she can outdo the lot of us, I'm telling you."

Mary beamed him a smile. "He only says that 'cause he knows I'll cook for him on the trail."

Amelia was amazed. Long's Peak stood some 14,700 feet high and butted itself in grand majesty against one end of Estes Park. It was once heralded as one of the noblest of the Rocky Mountains and Lady Bird had highly recommended taking the opportunity to ascend it, if time and health permitted one to do so. Amelia was still amazed that her father had taken to the idea without so much as a single objection. He and Sir Jeffery had found a guide to take them hunting outside the village area. They would be gone for over a week and during that time he was quite unconcerned with how his daughters and manservant entertained themselves. After all, he mused, they were quite well-chaperoned, everyone in the village clearly knowing what everyone else was about, and the isolation did not afford for undue notice of their activities by the outside world. Logan had immediately approached

114

him on the subject of Amelia ascending Long's Peak, with a formal invitation to include her sisters and the Gambett family. Lady Gambett looked as though just thinking of such a thing made her faint and the girls were clearly uninterested in anything so barbaric. After a brief series of questions, in which Mary assured the earl that she would look after Amelia as if she were her own, Lord Amhurst gave his consent and went off to clean his rifle. And that was that. The matter was settled almost before Amelia had known the question had been posed.

"You've got enough grub here to last three weeks," Jonas chided his wife.

"Sure, sure," his Mary answered with a knowing nod, "and you and Logan can eat three weeks worth of food in a matter of days. I intend that Amelia not starve." They all laughed at this and within the hour they were mounting their horses and heading out.

"Some folks call it 'the American Matterhorn'," Logan told Amelia.

"I've seen the Matterhorn and this is more magnificent," she replied, rather lost in thought.

The valley was a riot of colors and sights. The rich green of the grass contrasted with wildflowers too numerous to count. But thanks to Logan, Amelia could identify almost every one of them and smiled proudly at this inner knowledge. She would have quite a collection to show off when she returned to England. For reasons beyond her understanding, the thought of leaving for England didn't seem quite as appealing as it always had before. She pushed aside this thought and concentrated instead on the grandeur of a blue mountain lake that seemed to be nestled in a bed of green pine.

The Lewises' dogs, a collie mix and a mutt of unknown parentage, ran circles around the party, barking at everything that crossed their path, often giving chase when the subject in question looked too small to retaliate. Amelia laughed at the way they seemed to never tire of chasing the mountain ground squirrels or nipping after the heels of the mule-eared deer.

As the sun seemed to fall from the sky in an afterglow of evening colors, Amelia felt a sadness that she couldn't explain. The emptiness within her was almost more than she could bear. She thought of her mother and wondered if she were watching from some celestial home somewhere, then shook off the thought and chided herself for such imaginings. No doubt they'd been placed there by the irritating conversations of one Logan Reed. His beliefs seemed to saturate everything he said and did, and Amelia was quite disturbed by the way he lived this faith of his.

"We'd best make camp for the night," Logan called and pointed. "Over there looks to be our best choice."

Later, Amelia could see why he was so highly regarded as a competent guide. The area he'd chosen was well-sheltered from the canyon winds and had an ample supply of water. Added to this were feathery pine boughs, so surprisingly soft that when Amelia lay down atop her blanketed pine mattress, she sighed in unexpected delight. Staring up at the starry sky, Amelia uncomfortably remembered Bible verses from the thirty-eighth chapter of Job. Her mother had been particularly fond of these and had often quoted them when Amelia had questioned the 'how's' and 'why's' of God's workings.

"Where wast thou when I laid the foundations of the earth? declare, if thou hast understanding. Who hath laid the measures thereof, if thou knowest? or who hath stretched the line upon it? Whereupon are the foundations thereof fastened? or who laid the corner stone thereof; When the morning stars sang together, and all the sons of God shouted for joy?"

Her mother's explanation had always been that Amelia had no right to question God, and Amelia remembered countering that if God's position wasn't secure enough to be put to the test, then He wasn't as omnipotent and omniscient as people said. Suddenly, she felt very sorry for those words. Not because she believed in God's existence, but for the sorrow she remembered seeing in her mother's eyes. Sitting up, she hugged her knees to her chest and watched the flames of their campfire for awhile.

You wouldn't be very pleased with me now, Mother, she thought. The flames danced and licked at the cold night air and when a log popped and shifted, Amelia jumped from the suddenness of it.

"I'm surprised you're still awake," Logan said, from where he lay watching her.

Amelia felt suddenly very self-conscious and shrugged her shoulders. "Just thinking."

Logan leaned up on his elbow. "Care to share it?"

Amelia smiled and the reassuring sounds of Mary and Jonas' snoring made her relax a bit. "I was thinking about my mother."

"I bet you miss her a lot," Logan offered.

"Yes, I do. It seems like she's been gone forever and it's only been six years. She was sick quite awhile before she died." Then as if Logan had vocalized the question, Amelia added, "Consumption."

"And she was a Christian?"

Amelia rocked back and forth a bit and looked up to the heavens. "Yes."

"So how is it that you came to believe there was no God?"

"He never listened when I prayed," she replied flatly.

"How do you know?"

"Because my mother died."

Logan said nothing for several moments, then sat up and added a few more pieces of wood to the fire. "Did your mother ever deny you something that you wanted?"

"Of course," Amelia said, not understanding his meaning.

"So why wouldn't God be inclined to do the same?"

Logan's eyes were intense and his expression so captivating that for a moment Amelia forgot to be offended. Instead she simply asked, "To what purpose? I was fourteen years old, my youngest sister was barely ten. To what purpose does a merciful God remove mothers from children?"

"Good question. Wish I had the answer."

Amelia felt instant disappointment. She'd fully expected one of those quaint Christian answers like, "God needed another angel for heaven." Or, "God had need of your mother elsewhere." Amelia knew better. Especially since she left three grieving children and a devastated husband.

"You seem taken aback," Logan said softly. "Did you expect me to tell you the mind of God?"

Amelia couldn't help but nod. "Most other Christians would have. They have their wonderful little answers and reasons for everything, and none of it ever makes sense. To me, if there were a God, He would be more logical than that. There would be a definite order and reason to things and of course, a purpose."

"And you think that's missing in our world?" Logan questioned seeming genuinely intrigued by the turn the conversation had taken.

But Amelia felt weary of it all. She was tired of seeking answers when she wasn't even sure what the questions were. She couldn't make sense of her life or of her mother's death, therefore, to cast her frustration aside seemed the only way to keep from going insane.

"I think," she said very softly, "that the world has exactly the order we give it. No more. No less. If people are out of control, then so too, the world."

"I agree."

"You do?"

Logan smiled. "Surprised?" Amelia nodded and he continued. "God gave mankind free will to choose Him or reject Him. A great many folks refuse Him and chaos and misery ensue. They seek their own way and call it wisdom when they settle in their minds how the universe has come together."

"But is your Christianity any different? Didn't you decide in your own way how the universe has come together?"

"No," Logan replied. "I decided to accept that God's way was the only way and that put the rest of my questions at rest."

"But don't you ever worry that you might be wrong?" Amelia asked, knowing that she was very concerned with her own version of the truth. Perhaps that was why she felt herself in a constant state of longing. There was an emptiness inside her that refused to be filled up by the reasonings and logic of her own mind, yet she didn't know what to put in its place.

Logan stretched back on his pallet. "I guess if I'd come to God as an adult, I might have wondered if the Bible was true and if God was really God. But I became a Christian when I was still very young and it was easy to believe what my parents told me about the Bible and faith. I can see where it would be a whole heap harder for you. You have a lifetime of pride and obstacles to overcome. Accepting that the Bible is true would mean that your life would change, and some folks aren't willing to risk what that change might entail."

He fell silent and before long, Amelia noticed that his breathing had grown deep and even. Lying back down on her own pine bed, Amelia felt more lonely and isolated than she'd ever been in her life. *What if Logan was right?* her mind questioned. She quickly pushed the thought away. But as she drifted to sleep it came back in a haunting reminder that followed her even into her dreams.

The next day, Amelia awoke before it was fully light. The night had turned cold and Amelia's teeth chattered as she dragged her blankets around her shoulders and went to throw more wood on the fire like she'd seen Logan do. The dying coals quickly ignited the dry wood and soon a cheery blaze was crackling once again. It was this and not any sound made by Amelia which caused the rest of the camp to stir.

Logan was first to sit up, rubbing his eyes and yawning. Mary and Jonas murmured good mornings to each other before Mary took herself off for a bit of privacy. Jonas didn't seem inclined to talk and Logan was already pulling out things for breakfast.

While they were all occupied, Amelia took herself off a ways in order to study the sunrise in private. At first the blackness gave way to midnight blue and then as the slightest hint of lemon coloring suggested light, it gave way to a turquoise and brightened as the sun stretched over the snow-capped peaks. *How beautiful!* She marveled at the glory of it all.

They quickly breakfasted and were on their way by seven, the sunrise permanently fixed in Amelia's mind. They made good time, passing an area Logan called "The Lava Beds." It was here that huge boulders mingled with small ones to create a strangely desolate stage. They were nearing the place where Logan had said they would have to picket the horses and climb, when dark clouds moved in and rain appeared imminent.

Logan immediately went to work to find them even the smallest shelter to wait out the storm. He finally found a suitable place where they would be snug under the protective ledge of a particularly wide rock shelf. Jonas and Logan picketed the horses, while Amelia and Mary carried their things to the rock. The heavens opened up, as if cued by their having found shelter, and poured down a rain of tremendous proportion. Lightning flashed around them just as Jonas and Logan came to join the women.

C-R-A-C-K! Thunder roared, causing Amelia to nearly jump out of her skin. It seemed as if they sat atop the world and the fullest impact of the storm was to be spent on them alone.

Logan grinned, and eased a little closer to Amelia. Another flash of lightning caused Amelia to put her hands to her ears and press herself tighter to the wall. She felt terribly embarrassed by her childish display, noting that Mary and Jonas had their heads together talking as though nothing at all was amiss. She rallied herself in spirit and was determined to display more courage when a blinding strike of lightning hit directly in front of them with its deafening boom of thunder.

Amelia shrieked and threw herself at Logan in such a way that she feared she'd knocked the wind from him. Hearing him groan, she pulled back quickly, but found his arm around her.

"Stay, if it makes you feel better. I promise, Mary and Jonas aren't going to care."

Amelia smiled weakly at Mary. "I've never been in a storm like this," she said, barely able to form audible words.

"Logan knows how they go," Mary replied, which seemed to offer Amelia approval for her actions.

Turning to Logan, Amelia temporarily forgot the storm around her and concentrated instead on the one in his eyes. Her heart pounded harder, while her breath felt as though it were caught around the lump in her throat. Licking her dry lips, she eased away and hugged her arms around her. *Better to find strength and comfort from within than to lose another portion of myself to this rugged mountain man.*

After a time the storm passed, but Logan judged by the

skies that another would soon follow and the climb to the top of Long's Peak was postponed. As they descended back down the mountain, hoping to reach the heavy cover of pines before the next storm was upon them, Logan tried to treat the matter light-heartedly.

"We'll just try again later on," he said confidently. "Sooner or later, we're bound to get you to the top."

Amelia tried not to be disappointed. In truth, by this time her emotions were so topsy-turvy that she wasn't at all certain whether she cared if the trip were canceled or not. She rode sedately, saying very little except when addressed with a direct question. There was a great deal this trip had brought to mind and there was still the rest of the summer to think it through.

twelve

From that day, the summer passed much more quickly than Amelia had expected. Not a moment went by when she wasn't painfully aware that soon the snows would threaten to close off access to the plains. Soon she would be headed back to England and her marriage to Sir Jeffery. She tried to push down her fear, but it rose up like a phoenix from the ashes of her heart, threatening to slay her in mind and soul.

Her joy came in spending her days with Logan. With her father and Jeffery absorbed in their hunting and her sisters busy with the Gambett girls, Amelia found herself free to work with Mary each morning and then with Logan. She had copied down nearly every specimen of vegetation in the area, and Logan had taught her how to identify animal tracks and to mark her position from the village using the elements around her. She thought it almost her imagination, but swore her hearing had become better as she could make out sounds in the forested mountains that she'd never heard before. One day, when their water ran out, Logan had taught her how to listen for the sounds of water. Once she learned what it was that she was trying to hear, Amelia was amazed. The sounds had always been there, but she was just unaware of them. Before, the sounds in the air had come to her as a collective noise, but now she could separate the trickling of a mountain stream from the rustling of aspen leaves.

She had learned to depend more upon her other senses as well. Her sight and sense of smell were two things Logan said were absolutely necessary for staying alive. As they traipsed through the woods together he would often stop her and ask what certain smells were, and Amelia was quite proud to find that she was rapidly learning to identify each of these as well. Without realizing it, Amelia had spent the summer learning how to survive in the Rockies.

The bittersweetness of her circumstance, however, caught up with her one afternoon when her father sought her out.

"Amelia, we need to talk."

She looked up from where she was jotting down notes on a strange little bird which she had mistaken for a woodpecker.

"Just a moment Father," she said, finishing her notes. "I've identified that pesky noise we've lived with these months. You know that pecking sound that comes at all hours of the day and night?" She didn't wait for him to reply. "It seems that this bird is a chipping sparrow and it chips away all the time. It actually feeds its young even into adulthood when they are fully capable of feeding themselves. Isn't that fascinating?" This time she put the pen down and looked up to find her father's serious expression.

"Quite," was all he would reply on the matter before taking a seat across from her. "Amelia, you have sorely neglected the one duty I gave you—which was to allow Sir Jeffery to pay you court. I say, I've never seen a more stubborn woman in all my life, unless of course it was your mother."

Amelia smiled. "A high compliment if ever there was one."

The earl shook his head. "I'm afraid it wasn't intended as one. See here, I know how you feel about being forced to marry, but the truth is I can't have the family coffers being depleted because of your foolishness. Why any reasonable solicitor would allow your grandmother to set out a trust to unmarried daughters is beyond me. Why it positively reeks of inappropriateness."

"It was Grandmama's money, after all, and she was only

worried that her family might find themselves in situations of desperation and heartache. Grandmama had found it necessary to marry a man she didn't love, and all for financial reasons. She didn't want the same fate to befall her daughter or her granddaughters, yet now you propose to do just such a thing in order to keep the money for yourself." Amelia knew the anger in her heart was rapidly flooding over into her tone of voice.

"You have no right to speak to me thusly," the earl said rather stiffly. "I have to do what I feel is right for the benefit of the entire family, not just one member."

Amelia shook her head. "No, Father, I believe you are considering only one member—yourself." She slammed her book shut, mindless of smearing the still damp ink. "I've tried to be orderly about this and I've tried not to bring you undue pain, but I must speak honestly here." She swallowed hard and thought of the conversation she'd overheard her father having with Jeffery the night before. Logan would chide her for eavesdropping, but this time it served to clarify the mystery behind her father's desperation to marry her to Jeffery.

"I know about your gambling debts," she began, "and the fact that you owe Sir Jeffery a great deal of money." The earl's eyes widened in surprise. "I'm not the simpleton you would give me credit for being. It wasn't hard to learn about this, nor was it difficult to learn that you had promised Jeffery land in Scotland, land I might add which has been in our family for generations and which must pass through the succession of marriage or death, rather than be sold.

"Furthermore, I know that Jeffery covets the land for his own purposes, some known to me and others I'm sure are unknown, but nevertheless he wants that land. So now we come to the inheritance my grandmother set in place, Pan inheritance which passed to my mother and made the prospects of marrying beneath our status not quite so distasteful."

The earl pounded his fists on the table. "Enough! You know very well that I loved your mother and she loved me. Ours was not a marriage for fortune and status and you know well how the name of Amhurst suffered for just such impropriety."

Amelia took a deep breath and sighed. "Yes, but I must ask if it wasn't worth it?"

Lord Amhurst said nothing for a moment. His expression fell and he too sighed. "I could lie and say that if given the choice to do it all over again, I would marry another woman. But the truth is, I loved your mother very much and I would not trade our time together."

"So why are you trying to force such a thing upon me? If I were to inherit my share of the trust, do you believe I would leave you to suffer? How heartless you must think me."

"Nay, I never thought you heartless, but your share of the trust would never pay back what I owe Chamberlain. I'm sorry, Amelia." His resolve seemed to return. "You will have to marry Sir Jeffery."

Amelia felt as though a noose were being slipped around her neck. She rose with as much dignity as she could muster. "Your foolishness, not mine, has caused this situation. I find it completely unreasonable that I should be the one to pay for your mistakes. Let Jeffery marry one of my sisters. They both seem quite head-over-heels in love with the man."

Her father shook his head. "He wants the land which is to pass to you, Amelia. It is the Scottish estate which passes to the eldest that appeals to him."

"So I am to be sold off for the price of land and the sum of gambling debts?"

"Call it what you will," her father replied in a voice that suggested deep regret, "but avail yourself to Sir Jeffery in a proper courting manner and settle your mind on the fact that this marriage will take place."

&

Later that week while dressing quietly for dinner, Amelia felt a desperation building inside that couldn't be cast away with the assurance that she'd somehow work things around to her way. Jeffery had lost little time in picking up his pursuit of Amelia and as his attentions became bolder, Amelia was forced to sequester herself in her cabin for fear of what he might do next.

Penelope and Margaret were already talking of returning home and of all the things they would do. Amelia tried to remember her own earlier desires to return to England, but they'd passed from existence and now she wanted instead to remain in Estes. It was almost humorous to her that in the three months they'd spent in America, and Estes in particular, her views about the barbaric ways of the Americans had changed. She had come to look at Mary as a mother image and she cherished the time spent under her tutelage. She'd learned to cook and bake, as well as sew practical garments and quilt. Mary had also shown her how to properly clean house and wash clothes. And when time permitted, Amelia had even taken lessons in tending the vegetable garden and livestock.

As she pulled on her gloves for dinner she looked at her hands and realized how worn and rough they'd become. Back in England her friend Sarah would be appalled at the sight of calluses upon a lady's fingers, but Amelia wore them as badges of honor. She'd earned those calluses by working at Mary's side and she was proud of what she'd accomplished.

"Oh do hurry, Amelia," Penelope whined. "We'll never be able to sit down to dinner if you don't finish getting ready."

"I for one, refuse to wait," Margaret said, grabbing her

shawl. "Come along, sister. Amelia will bring herself when she's ready. Maybe we can corner Sir Jeffery and he'll tell us more tales of his adventures in China."

"Oh yes," Penelope said, nodding her head. "That would be grand."

They left Amelia in a rush of chatter and anticipation of the night to come. She stared after them through the open door and shook her head. If only she could feel such enthusiasm for Sir Jeffery, none of this might have ever happened. The afterglow of sunset left a haunting amber color to the sky over the mountains. The chill of autumn was approaching and with it came a longing that Amelia could not explain. If only they had never come to America she would never have laid eyes on the Rocky Mountains and never have met Logan Reed.

Logan.

Her heart ached from the very thought of his name. She was hopelessly in love with him, and yet, there was nothing to be done about it. Logan was as poor as a church mouse and he could never offer to pay off her father's debts the way Jeffery could. Her father owed Jeffery over seventy-thousand pounds and even with her trust, the debt would barely be half paid. It was rapidly becoming a hopeless state of circumstances.

"Well, well," Jeffery announced from the door. "I looked about for you and found you missing."

"With good reason," Amelia said rather angrily. "I wasn't yet ready to present myself at dinner."

Jeffery leered. "I could help you. . .dress."

"As you can see, I'm quite dressed and I suggest you keep your disgusting thoughts to yourself."

She moved across the room to retrieve her shawl and heard Jeffery close the cabin door. Turning around, she found that he'd already crossed the room. He took hold of her roughly and crushed her against him in a fierce embrace.

"Stop it, Jeffery!" she declared and pushed at his chest.

Jeffery only laughed and held her fast. "You mustn't put me off. We're to be man and wife after all. A kiss of passion shared between two lovers is quite acceptable."

"But you forget. I do not love you," Amelia answered, kicking Jeffery's shin as hard as she could.

He immediately released her and Amelia scurried from the room, panting for breath and close to tears. Jeffery had so frightened her with his actions that she was quite uncertain as to what she should do next. Fleeing into the darkness behind the lodge, Amelia waited until her breathing had calmed and her heart stopped racing. *What should I do? What can I do?* Her father had made it quite clear and there was no other answer. She waited several more minutes, knowing that she was keeping everyone from their meal, then with a sigh she went to face them all. Walking slowly, as if to her own execution, Amelia entered the lodge and the dining hall without the slightest desire to be among people.

"Ah, there she is now," Lord Amhurst announced. "Amelia, dear, come and join us in a toast."

Amelia looked up and found the entire party staring at her. Everyone seemed quite joyous and Jeffery stood with an expression of sheer pride on his face. They weren't apparently unhappy with her for the delay of their dinner and instead seemed extremely animated.

"What, might I ask, are we drinking a toast to?" she asked, hesitantly.

The earl beamed a smile upon her. "Sir Jeffery has told us that this night you have accepted his hand in marriage." Her father raised his drink. "We are drinking to you and Sir Jeffery and a long, happy marriage."

Amelia felt the wind nearly knocked from her. She looked from her father to Jeffery and found a sneering grin on his face. His expression seemed to say, "I told you I would have my way."

"Well, do come join us," her father said, rather anxiously. "We've waited all summer for this."

Amelia found it impossible to speak. A lump formed in her throat and tears were threatening to spill from her eyes. Without concern for appearances, she turned and ran from the lodge.

Fleeing down the stairs and into the night, Amelia barely stifled a scream as she ran full-speed into Logan Reed's arms. She couldn't see his face, but heard his chuckle and felt a sense of comfort in just knowing he was near.

"I'm so sorry," she said, trying to disentangle her arms from his.

"I'm not. Want to tell me what you were running from?" Amelia felt the tears trickle down her cheeks and a sob escaped her throat. Logan's voice grew more concerned. "What is it Amelia? What has happened?"

"Nothing," she said, unable to keep from crying.

He took hold of her upper arms. "You're crying, so something must be wrong."

"Just leave me alone."

His voice was low and husky. "Amelia, I care about your pain and so does God. He can help you through this, even if I can't."

She jerked away, angry at the suggestion. "If God cares so much about pain, then why does He let His children suffer? I'm going to my cabin," she declared and walked away.

Logan was quickly at her side and it wasn't until she'd opened the door to her still lighted cabin that she could see that he was smiling.

"What? Are you going to laugh at me now?"

"Not at all. It's just that I thought you didn't believe in God."

"I don't."

"Then why did you say what you did about God letting His children suffer."

"Because you are always throwing your religion and God in my face!" she declared. "You always fall back on that and always use that to settle every issue that has ever arisen between us."

"Because He is my foundation and my mainstay. God cares about your pain, but haven't you brought it on yourself? Don't you hold any responsibility for your own actions?"

"Oh, go away, Logan," she moaned in sheer misery. *Why did he have to say those things?*

With a shrug of his shoulders, Logan surprised her by turning to leave. "I'm gonna pray for you Amelia. I know you're having a rough time of coming to terms with God, but just remember, He already knows what's in your heart and He knows the future He holds for you."

With that, he was gone and Amelia closed the door to cry in earnest. *Why is this happening to me and what in the world am I to do about any of it?* Giving up on the world and conscious thought, Amelia stripped off her dinner clothes and pulled on a nightgown. Then, mindless of her sisters, she blew out the lamp and threw herself into bed to have a good long cry.

thirteen

"Well, if you ask me," Penelope began, "I think it positively scandalous the way you put Sir Jeffery off."

"No one asked you," Amelia said flatly. She busied herself with quilting and tried to ignore her sisters and the Gambett girls.

"Mother says it is outrageous for you to suppose you will get a better match than Sir Jeffery," Josephine Gambett said, pushing up her glasses. They immediately slid back down her nose.

"Yes, Mother believes you are seriously jeopardizing your family's position with the Queen. After all, Sir Chamberlain's mother is a dear friend of Her Majesty," Henrietta added, not to be outdone by her sister.

Amelia felt her cheeks burn from the comeuppance of these younger girls. She thought of a hundred retorts, but bit her tongue and continued stitching.

"I think it's pure selfishness on your part," Margaret said with a little stomp of her foot. "There are other people to consider in this situation."

Amelia finally set aside her quilting and looked hard at each of the girls. "If you'll excuse me, I believe I would prefer the company of adults." With that she got up and without any conscious plan to do so, made her way to the cabin her father shared with Mattersley. She knew he would be there cleaning his guns and in her mind she formed one last plan to plead her case.

"Father?" she said, knocking lightly upon the open door.

Mattersley shuffled across the room. His face looked

pinched and his eyes were sunken. "Come in, Lady Amhurst. The earl is just now occupied with the weapons."

Amelia smiled at him. Even here in the wilds of America, Mattersley held to the strict code of English propriety. "Thank you, Mattersley." She started to walk past him then stopped and asked, "How are you feeling? You look a bit tired."

Mattersley seemed stunned by her concern. "I am well, Miss."

"You should have some time off to yourself," she said, glancing to where her father sat. "Father, don't you agree?"

"Say what?" the earl questioned, looking up.

"I believe Mattersley is working too hard and some time off would serve him well."

"Oh, well yes," her father said, genuinely seeming to consider this. "A capital idea! Mattersley, you go right ahead and take the rest of the day—"

"No," Amelia interrupted, "a day will certainly not afford him much of a rest. I suggest the rest of the week. He can stay up in the lodge. I know Mary has extra room."

"Oh." Her father seemed quite taken aback.

"There is no need for that, Sir," Mattersley said in a voice that betrayed his weariness.

"My daughter is quite right," Lord Amhurst answered, seeming to see the old man for the first time. "You've been out on nearly every hunt with us and working to keep my things in order. I can surely dress myself properly enough for the rest of the week, what?"

"Very good, Sir," Mattersley replied and Amelia thought it almost sounded like a sigh of relief.

"Well, now that this matter has been resolved," she began and took the chair beside her father, "I thought we might address another."

"Do tell?" the earl replied and continued with cleaning his shotgun.

"Father, I have come to plead with you one final time to release me from this preposterous suggestion that I marry Sir Jeffery." The earl said nothing and so Amelia continued. "I cannot marry a man I do not respect, and I hold not the slightest respect for Sir Jeffery. I also cannot bring myself to consider marrying a man I do not love."

"Such modern notions do you a grave injustice, my dear," her father replied. "My mind is set and this is my final word. You will marry Chamberlain. In fact, I've arranged for us to depart Estes in three weeks. We will travel by stage from Greeley to Denver and there you will be married."

"What! How can you suggest such a thing? Why that won't even allow for a proper wedding, much less a proper English wedding," Amelia protested.

"It is of little concern. Sir Jeffery and I discussed the matter and we both believe it to be to the benefit of both parties."

"What parties? You and Jeffery? Because, I assure you it will never be to my benefit." She got to her feet, trembling from her father's declaration. "I cannot understand how my own father would sell me into such an abominable circumstance."

"And I cannot imagine that I raised a daughter to be so defiant and disobedient," the earl replied, looking at her with a stern expression of dismay. "Your mother would not be pleased in the way you've turned out. Even she would find your temperament to be unwarranted."

"Mother would understand," Amelia said softly, the anger being quickly replaced by the realization that her father could care less about her feelings. "And once, when you and she were still together, you would have understood too."

She left the cabin and felt as though a damp, cold blanket had been thrust upon her shoulders. The weight of her father's sudden declaration was more than she'd even imagined him capable of turning out. Immediately her mind sought for some manner of refuge. *There has to be something I can do.*

She walked a ways up the mountain side and paused beside a formation of boulders and rock. Hiking up her skirt, she climbed to the top by inching her way along the crevices and hand-holds. Once she'd managed to achieve her goal, she sat down in complete dejection and surveyed the village below.

Three weeks was a very short time.

She sighed and thought of leaving Estes and knew that it was tearing at her in a way that she'd never prepared herself for. She would have to leave the clean, crisp mountain air and the beauty that she'd never grow tired of looking upon. *And for what? To return to the cold, damp English winters? To be the wife of that unbearably cruel bore?*

She felt a tear trickle down her cheek and rubbed it away with the back of her sleeve. She almost laughed at herself for the crude gesture. *In so many ways I've become one of them. How can I go back to England now?*

"I can't do it," she whispered. "I can't go back."

That left her with very few alternatives. She couldn't very well talk her father into letting her remain in America. Soon enough she would be twenty-one and her father would never allow that day to come without her being properly married to Sir Jeffery.

"I could run away," she murmured and the thought suddenly seemed very possible. *Logan has taught me how to find my way around,* she reasoned. *I could hide out in the mountains until after my birthday and then Father would have no choice.* But her birthday was the twenty-third of November and by that time this entire area would be snow-packed and frightfully cold. There was no way she would survive.

"But I don't want to survive if I have to marry Jeffery."

With that declaration an entirely different thought came to mind. Taking her own life could not be ruled out as a possible alternative. She thought of Crying Rock and the Indian maid who'd bravely gone to her death rather than face the unbearable ordeal of marrying a man she abhorred. *I'm no different than that woman. My sorrow is certainly well-founded. To leave this place, this lovely, wonderful place would be sheer misery.* And yet, even as she thought it, Amelia knew it wasn't just the place—it was Logan. Marriage to any man other than Logan was simply unthinkable.

"But he doesn't feel the same way I do," she chided. "He has his God and his religion and he doesn't need a woman who would fight him with intellectual words and philosophies." *No, Logan needs a wife who would work at his side, worship at his side, raise a family at his side. Logan would expect her to believe as he did, that God not only existed, but that He played an intricate role in the lives of His children. And that in doing so, He gave them a Savior in Jesus Christ.*

Something her mother had once said came back to haunt her. "Only the foolish man believes there is no God, Amelia. For the Bible says, 'even the demons believe in God, and they tremble'."

Amelia gazed out over the valley and sighed. Logan said she had but to open her eyes to the handiwork of God to realize His existence. But how could she believe in God, much less in the need to worship Him and follow all manner of rule and regulation laid out in the Bible? To what purpose was there such a belief as the need for eternal life? Wasn't it just that mortal man could not stand to believe that his important life ended in the grave? Wasn't the idea of immortality something mankind comforted itself with in lieu of facing the truth that once you died, that was all there was? After all, most religions she'd studied had some form of immortality for their believers. It was rather like a parting gift from a high-society soiree. Something to cherish for those who had the courage to play the party games.

"I do not need such comfort," she whispered and hugged her arms close. "When my life is done, it is done and there will be no marriage to Sir Jeffery and no longing for what I can never have."

Suddenly it seemed quite reasonable to put an end to her life. In fact, it was almost calming. If there was nothing else to concern herself with, why not stop now? She'd seen more of the world than most people. She'd enjoyed the pleasures of the privileged life and she'd once known the love of good parents and siblings. *So what if I never know the love of a man—never know the joys of motherhood?* She wiped the tears which were now pouring freely from her eyes.

"I will go to Jeffery and plead my case before him. I will tell him honestly that I have no desire to marry him and suggest to him a different course," she told the valley before her. She climbed down from the rock and smoothed her skirt. "If he refuses to give consideration to my desires, then the matter will be resolved for me."

She thought that there should be some kind of feeling of accomplishment in making such a decision, but there wasn't. She felt empty and void of life. "I am resigned to do this thing," she said as an encouragement to her broken spirit. "There is no other way."

fourteen

"Sir Jeffery, I wonder if I might have a moment of your time," Amelia began one evening after dinner.

He seemed to sneer down his nose at her as though her request had somehow reduced her to a beggar. "I would be honored," he said and extended his arm for her.

Amelia, seeing all faces turned to behold her action, placed her hand upon his sleeve. "I suggest a short walk, if that would meet with your approval," she said cautiously.

"But of course, Lady Amhurst. I am your servant."

Amelia said nothing more, but allowed Jeffery to lead her amicably from the lodge.

"I must say this is a pleasant surprise. Dare I hope you're coming around to my way of thinking?"

Amelia let go of him and shook her head. "No, rather I was hoping to persuade you to my way of thinking."

"How so?"

"Sir Jeffery, I have no desire to marry you. I do not love you and I never will. I cannot make it any clearer on this point." She turned to him in the dim lamp light of the porch and hoped he would understand. "I know about your hold on Father and I know about your desire for the Scottish property." She held up her hand to wave off his question. "I overheard you two discussing the matter one evening. Therefore, I know, too, that you are not marrying me because of any great love, but rather because you want a good turn of business."

"Fair enough," Jeffery replied and leaned back against the porch railing. "But your knowing the circumstance does nothing to change my decision."

"But why not? Why not be an honorable man about this and allow Father some other means by which to settle his debt?"

"I'm open to other means. If you can put the seventy-thousand pounds in my hand, I'll call the entire wedding off."

"Truly?" she asked, feeling at once hopeful.

Jeffery sneered and laughed. "But of course, you can't put that kind of money in my hands, even if you inherit, can you?"

"Perhaps not right away, but I could put over half of it in your hands."

"What? And leave yourself with no income. If you do not marry, your father is sure to exile you to that pitifully cold Scottish estate you seem so inclined to hang on to. Without funds, how do you propose to live?"

"I hope to sell my book when we return to England. Lady Bird suggested—"

"No, Amelia. I will not call off this wedding on your hopes and the suggestions of Lady Bird."

"And there is no other way to convince you?"

"None. Now stop being such a foolish child about it all. You'll have the very best of everything, I assure you. And, if you're concerned about your freedom to find true love, I will even go so far as to say that as long as you are discrete about your affairs, I will be most tolerant of them."

Amelia was totally aghast. "I would never consider such a thing!"

Jeffery sighed and spoke tolerantly as though dealing with a simpleton. "It is done all the time, Amelia dear. Most of nobility take lovers because they've been forced into love-less marriages. I'm simply trying to offer you what would be an acceptable arrangement in lieu of your sacrificing to a marriage of arrangement."

Noises from the front of the lodge porch told Amelia that her sisters and their friends were making their way over to the Amhurst cabin. They were giggling and talking in rapid fire succession about some point or another. It probably amounted to nothing more than their ritual game of after-dinner whist. Amelia lowered her voice to avoid drawing attention to herself.

"I am appalled that you would suggest such a thing. Marriage is a sacred institution, not something to be flaunted about and infringed upon by numerous affairs."

"My dear, you are quite naive to believe such a thing. I had thought you to be more mature about these matters, especially in light of your disbelief in holy affairs. I thought you above all other women to be removed from such nonsense."

"Faithfulness has never been nonsense to my way of thinking."

"Ah, but it is your way of thinking that is keeping this matter unresolved. Your father has made up his mind to accept my generous offer. It will benefit all people in one way or another. Yes, even you will benefit, Amelia, and if you would but stop to think about it, you would see that I speak the truth. You might even come to enjoy my company after a time, and furthermore, to find pleasure in my bed."

Amelia dismissed such notions with her coldest stare. She hoped Jeffery felt frozen to the bone from her look. "I believe we've said all there is to say," she stated and turned to leave. Jeffery did nothing to stop her.

"You'll soon see for yourself, Amelia," he called after her, then laughed in a way that suggested he was very much enjoying the entire matter.

Amelia hurried to her cabin, fighting back tears and angry retorts. She knew that there was little to be done but accept her fate. Suicide seemed her only answer and her heart grew even heavier as she considered how she might accomplish such a fate.

"I want to wear the green one," Penelope argued and pulled the gown from Margaret's hold. Both sisters looked up guiltily as Amelia entered the room to find them fighting over her gowns.

When Amelia remained fixed in her place, saying nothing of reprimand, Penelope took the opportunity to explain. "There is to be a dance tonight. They're clearing the lodge's main room and Mary is fixing refreshments. It won't be as nice as a fancy ball, but I'm positively dying to dance. And Mr. Reed said the local men will come and serve as partners."

Margaret lifted her nose in the air and said, "I do hope they bathe. Some of these Americans seem not to know what a benefit water and soap can be." Her attitude suggested she might be reconsidering her appearance at the dance, but just when Amelia figured her to be absent, Margaret's expression changed to one of pleading desperation. "You simply must let us borrow your dresses. You have so many pretty gowns that you've not even worn and we've only those old things." She waved to a small stack of discarded gowns.

"Do whatever you like," Amelia finally said in a voice of pure resignation. "You may have all of my dresses for all I care. I won't be needing them anymore."

"You're only saying that to make me feel bad," Penelope said, puffing out her chest indignantly. "Just because you are marrying Sir Jeffery in Denver and will receive a new trousseau, you think you can be cruel."

"Yes, you are very mean-spirited, Amelia," Margaret agreed. "I think I've never met a more hateful person. You'll have Sir Jeffery and his money and go to court and spend your days in all the finery and luxury money can buy. We'll still be trying to make a proper match."

"Yes," Penelope added with a sigh, "and hoping that our husbands will be as handsome and rich as Sir Jeffery." Both of them broke into tittering giggles before Penelope sobered and tightened her hold on the gown as though Amelia might change her mind. "So you needn't be so smug Amelia. You may walk around with your nose in the air for all we care."

Amelia looked at them both. She was stunned by their harshness and hurt by their comments. These were her sisters and there had been a time when they were all close and happy. She remembered joyous times when they were little and she'd played happily with them in the nursery. She loved them, even if they couldn't see that. Even if time and sorrow had made them harsh, and strained their ability to be kind. She saw hints of their mother woven in their expressions. Margaret looked like their mother more than any of them, but even Penelope shared a similar mouth and nose. Amelia sighed. They should be close, as close as any three people could ever be. But they thought her a snob and a spiteful, prideful person, and perhaps they were right. It seemed only to fuel the idea that the world would be a better place without her in it.

Not wishing to leave them with a bitter memory of her, she offered softly, "I do apologize. I fear you have misjudged me, however. It was never my intentions to make you feel bad."

Margaret and Penelope looked at her in complete surprise. Amelia wondered if they had any idea of what she was about to do. They were so young and childish and probably concerned themselves only with what color would best highlight their eyes or hair. No doubt they prayed fervently that Amelia would allow Jeffery the freedom to dance with them and pay them the attention they so craved. *Will they mourn me when I am gone? Will anyone?*

"You don't care at all how we feel. All summer you've pranced around here like some sort of queen. Always you've had the best of everything and Father even allowed you to remain behind from the hunt when we had to drudge about this horrid country looking for sport!" Penelope declared.

"Yes, it's true!" Margaret exclaimed in agreement. "You had Jeffery's undivided attention and positively misused him. You have no heart, Amelia."

Amelia could no longer stand up under their criticism. She felt herself close to tears again and rather than allow them to see her cry, turned at the door to walk away. "You needn't worry about the matter any more," she called over her shoulder. "I'll take myself to the Crying Rock and relieve you of your miseries."

Crossing the yard, Amelia looked heavenward. A huge milky moon shone down to light her way and a million stars sparkled against the blackness. Mother had told her that stars were the candlelights of angels.

"But I can't see the angels, Mother," Amelia had said in her doubt and disbelief.

"We can't always see the good things at hand, but we can trust them to be there."

Amelia sighed and rubbed her arms against the chill. "You were wrong, Mother. There is no good thing at hand for me."

She made her way up the mountain through the heavy undergrowth of the forest floor. She only vaguely knew the path to the Crying Rock and hoped she'd find the right way. Tears blinded her from seeing what little moonlight had managed to filter down through the trees. She'd never been one given to tears, but during these few months in America she'd cried enough for a lifetime. Now, it seemed that her lifetime should appropriately come to an end.

Her sisters' harsh comments were still ringing in her ears

and her chest felt tight and constricted with guilt and anguish. *Perhaps they're right. Perhaps I am heartless and cruel. The world would be a much better place without me.*

God cares about your pain. Logan's words come back to mind so clearly that Amelia stopped in her place and listened for him to speak. The wind moaned through the trees and Amelia realized that it was nothing but her mind playing tricks on her. *There is no God,* she reminded herself, chiding herself for being foolish.

"Even if there were," she muttered, "He wouldn't care about me."

❧

Logan leaned against the stone wall of the fireplace and wondered if Amelia would join in the evening fun. He'd watched her from afar and saw that her mind was overly burdened with matters that she refused to share. He'd prayed for her to find the answers she longed for.

Over in one corner, Lord Amhurst and Sir Jeffery were steeped in conversation and Logan couldn't help but watch them with a feeling of contempt. *What kind of man forces his child to marry against her will? Especially a man who represents nothing but fearful teasing from childhood and snobbish formality in adulthood.* He longed to understand better and not to feel so judgmental about Amelia's father and his insistence that she wed Jeffery Chamberlain. He knew very little except for what he'd overheard and none of that gave him the full picture. He'd tried to get Amelia to talk about it, but even when he'd caught her in moments where she was less guarded about her speech, she refused to share her concerns with him.

His mind went back to the conversation he'd overheard earlier that evening between Amelia and Jeffery. He'd been coming to the lodge and rounded the back corner just in time to hear Amelia tell Chamberlain that she believed in faithfulness in marriage. Chamberlain certainly hadn't, but it didn't surprise Logan.

"Well, well, and here come some of our lovely ladies now," the earl stated loudly.

Logan looked up to find Amelia's sisters flouncing about the room in their finery. Lady Gambett and her daughters were quick to follow them into the room, but Amelia was nowhere to be found.

"I say, Penelope," Lord Amhurst began, "isn't that one of Amelia's gowns?"

Penelope whirled in the pale green silk. "Yes, Father, it is."

"You know how particular your sister is about her gowns. It will certainly miff her to find you in it."

"She knows all about it," Penelope replied.

"Yes, Father, she does. In fact, this is her gown also and she told me I could wear it," Margaret chattered. "Although it is a bit large."

Logan smiled, seeing for himself that Margaret's girlish figure couldn't quite fill out the bodice. He could imagine Amelia growing impatient with them both and throwing the gowns in their faces. Sipping a cup of coffee, Logan tried to hide his smile and keep his thoughts to himself.

In one corner, several of the boys were tuning up their fiddles and guitars to provide the evening's music, while the earl exchanged formalities with the newly arrived Lord Gambett. They talked for several minutes while the ladies gathered around Jeffery, each vying for his compliments. Some of the local men straggled in and Logan nearly laughed aloud at the way they each paused at the door to shine their boots on the backside of the opposite leg. Never mind their jeans might show a smudge of dirt, so long as their boots looked good. Logan almost felt sorry for them, knowing that these prim and proper English roses would hardly appreciate the effort.

"We're certain to beat the snow if we leave at the end of next week instead of waiting," Logan heard Lord Gambett say.

"What do say you, Mr. Reed? Is the snow upon us?" Lord Amhurst suddenly questioned.

"It's due, that's for sure," Logan replied. "But I think you're safe from any real accumulation. We might see a dusting here and there, but it doesn't look bad just yet. Of course, with mountain weather that could all change by morning."

The musicians were ready and awaited some kind of cue that they should begin playing. The fiddle player was already drawing his bow across the strings in what Logan knew to be an American-styled call to order. He looked around the room and still seeing no sign of Amelia, questioned the earl about beginning the music.

"I see Lady Amhurst is still absent, but if you would like, the boys are ready to begin playing."

The earl glanced around as though Amelia's absence was news. "I say, Penelope, where is that sister of yours? She doesn't seem to be here."

Penelope shrugged. "She left the cabin after telling us to wear whatever we wanted. She was mean-tempered and said she wouldn't be needing these gowns anymore. We presumed she said that because of her marriage to Sir Jeffery. Don't you think it mean of her to boast that way?"

Lord Amhurst laughed. "At least she's finally coming around to our way of thinking, what?" He elbowed Jeffery and laughed.

"Indeed it would appear that way," the sneering man replied.

Logan hated his smugness and thought of his lurid suggestion that Amelia would come to enjoy his bed. Logan seethed at the thought of Amelia joining this man in marriage. He had worked all week long to figure out what he could do to resolve Amelia's situation. He couldn't understand her loyalty to a father who would be so unconcerned with her feelings, and yet he respected her honoring him with obedience. *Somehow there has to be a way to make things right for Amelia.* He thought of approaching the earl and asking for Amelia's hand, but he was already certain that the man would never consider him a proper suitor, much less a proper husband.

"I congratulate you, Chamberlain, on your powers of persuasion. You must have given her a good talking to in order to convince her to marry."

"Maybe it was more than a talking to," Lady Gambett said in uncharacteristic fashion.

The girls all giggled and blushed at this. They whispered among themselves at just what such possibilities might entail, while Jeffery smiled smugly and accepted their suppositions. Logan barely held his temper and would have gladly belted the grin off Chamberlain's face had his attention not been taken in yet another startling direction.

"But did Amelia say when she might join us?" the earl asked, suddenly seeming to want to push the party forward.

"No," Penelope replied, "she said she was going off to cry on some rock. I suppose she'll be at it all night and come back with puffy red eyes."

"Then she'll be too embarrassed to come to the party," Margaret replied.

Logan felt his breath quicken and his mind repeated the words Penelope had just uttered. *"She said she was going off to cry on some rock."* Did she mean Crying Rock? He put his cup down and signaled the band to begin. He wanted no interference on exiting quickly and figured with the music as a diversion he could make his way out the back kitchen door.

He was right. Logan slipped from the room without anyone voicing so much as a "Good evening." His thoughts
haunted him as he made his way to the end of the porch. He
grabbed a lighted lantern as he jumped down from the steps.
*She doesn't want this marriage and she knows about Crying
Rock.* He mentally kicked himself for ever taking her there.

"Lord, if I've caused her to seek a way out that costs
Amelia her life, I'll never forgive myself," he muttered.

fifteen

As if drawn there by sheer will, Amelia finally made her way to Crying Rock. She stood for a moment under the full moon and looked down on the valley below. Across the mountains the moon's reflection made it appear as though it were day. The dark, shadowy covering of pine and aspen looked like an ink smudge against the valley. The mournful sound of the wind playing in the canyons seemed to join Amelia's sobs in sympathetic chorus.

Her gown of lavender crepe de Chine did little to ward off the bite of the mountain breeze. The polonaise styling with its full skirt and looped-up draping in back gave a bit of protection, but the wind seemed to pass right through the low cut bodice and was hardly deterred by the chiffon modesty scarf that she'd tucked into it. The finery of a Paris gown meant little to her now. *What good were such baubles when no one cared if you lived or died?*

She stepped closer to the edge and wiped her tear-stained face. *Father will be very unhappy when he learns what I've done. All of his plans will be for naught, and yet he'll still have his money and the land will pass to Penelope.* Perhaps her sister would go willingly into marriage with Sir Jeffery. Thinking of Jeffery made her stomach hurt. He was mean and crude and just standing over the dizzying drop made her remember his cruelty to her as a child.

"This thing must be done," she said to the sky and then sank to her knees in misery. *If only there were some reason to go on with life.* She simply couldn't see herself at Jeffery's side playing the innocent wife while keeping her lovers waiting in hidden rooms. Furthermore, to imagine that Jeffery would entertain himself in such a manner bothered her pride more than she could admit. If Jeffery had at least loved her, it might have been possible to go into the marriage. But he wanted nothing more than her father's money and the manipulative power to control all that she would inherit. Amelia felt sick just imagining the arrangement.

"If God did exist—" she said softly and lifted her gaze again to the panoramic view of the mountains. She thought of Logan and all that he'd shared with her about God and the Bible. She thought of his faith to believe in such matters. He was totally unwavering, even when she made what she knew was a strong argument against his beliefs. Logan wouldn't argue with her about God. And it wasn't because Amelia hadn't sought to stir up a conflict now and then. Logan would merely state what he believed to be the facts and leave Amelia to sort through it herself. She remembered one conversation which had taken place several days earlier in which she had asked Logan how he could be so certain that he was right in his beliefs.

"How can you be so certain that I'm not?" he had questioned. "I'm willing to bet my life on my beliefs. Are you?"

Amelia felt a chill run through her at the memory. Was she willing to bet her life on her beliefs? Her mother's faith had been the foundation for their household. Her father had even admitted that it was one of the things which had attracted him to her in the first place.

"Mother, why did you have to leave us?" Amelia whispered. "Why did you have to leave me with so many questions? If God loves us as you always said He did, then why did He cruelly take you from the children who needed you? Where is God's mercy in that? Where is the love?"

The rustlings of the wind in the trees below were all that came back in reply.

"All right," she said giving in to the tremendous longing in her soul. "If You exist God, then why do you allow such tragedy and injustice? Why, if You are such a loving Father, do You allow Your children to experience such pain?" she paused in questioning and rubbed her arms against the mountain chill. "Why do You allow *me* to hurt so much?"

"I want to believe," she said and this time the tears came. "I want to believe." She sobbed and buried her face in her hands. "But it hurts so much and I'm so afraid that You won't be any more constant than Mother was. If I believed, would You merely go away when I needed You most, just as she did?"

A verse of Scripture from childhood from the last chapter of Matthew, came to memory. "And, lo, I am with you always, *even* unto the end of the world."

"But the world is filled with a variety of beliefs and religious nonsense," Amelia protested against the pulling of her spirit. "How can I know that this is real? How can I know that I am choosing the right path?"

Logan had said it was a matter of faith and in believing that the Bible was truly the word of God. Logan had also said that God proved Himself over and over, even in the little day to day points of life.

"God, if You are real," Amelia said, lifting her face to the starry, moonlit sky overhead, "then You must show me in such a way that I cannot miss it in my blind foolishness."

But even if God was real He wouldn't change my plight. What tiny thread of hope had begun to weave itself through her broken heart, snapped with this sudden realization. She was still facing her father's edict that she marry a man she didn't care about. She would still find herself headed back to England within the month. And, she would still lose the man she loved.

Logan came to mind with such a powerful urgency that

Amelia no longer fought against it. She loved him as truly as she had ever loved anyone, and in many ways, intimate and frightening ways, she loved him more than she had ever loved anyone else. Logan was like no one else in the world. He cared to share his faith with her in such a way that it wasn't merely preaching for the sake of fulfilling his obligation to God—rather it was that his heart was so full to overflowing with love for his God and Savior that he couldn't help but share it.

Then too, Logan was perhaps the only man who had ever treated her with respect that didn't come from a sense of noble obligation. Logan spoke his mind and refused to play into her role of "Ladyship", but he also afforded her a kindness and gentleness of spirit that only her mother had ever given her. But of course, that didn't mean he loved her and love was truly all that Amelia longed for in life.

"There is no reason to live without it," she whispered. "Oh, God, if You are real then give me a reason to live. Send me love. Real and true love. Please, let someone love me," she sobbed.

"I love you," Logan said from somewhere behind her. "Even more, God loves you, Amelia."

The sound of his voice startled her so badly that Amelia hurried to her feet, tangling her skirt around her legs as she tried to straighten up. Caught off guard by Logan and by the gown's hold on her, Amelia lost her balance and fell to the ground. The impact caused a piece of the rocky ledge to give way and Amelia felt herself slipping from the safety of Crying Rock.

Digging her hands into the rock and dirt, she thought, *Not now. I can't die now!* But even as the thought crossed her mind, she was more than aware of her dangerous situation. With what she thought would surely be her last breath, she screamed Logan's name.

"Amelia!" he cried out from overhead. "I thought I'd lost you!"

She pressed her body against the cold, hard granite and for the first time in her life began to pray earnestly. She barely heard Logan calling her name and refused to even lift her face to search for him overhead.

"Amelia, you have to listen to me," Logan said again. "Can you hear me?"

"Yes." She barely breathed the word.

As he moved overhead, bits of rock and dirt pelted down on her head causing Amelia to shriek in fear. "Don't be scared, Amelia, I'll soon have you right as rain."

She would have laughed had the predicament not been so grave. *Don't be scared?* She was long past scared. She was terrified to the point that she thought she might pass out cold and end any hope of her rescue.

"Listen to me Amelia. I can reach your hand if you lift your arm up."

"No, I'm not moving," Amelia replied, hardly daring to breath.

"You have to do as I say or you may well be on that ledge for whatever time you have left on earth."

She said nothing for several heartbeats and then spoke in a barely audible voice. "I can't do it, Logan."

Logan seemed not to hear her. "Look up and to your right. I'm reaching down as far as I can and I can almost touch your head. All you have to do is give me your hand. I promise I won't let you go."

"I can't do it," she repeated sternly.

"Yes, you can," he told her sounding so confident that she felt a surge of hope. "Trust me, Amelia. Have faith in me and what God can do."

Amelia felt the pounding of her heart and the fierce chill of the wind as it whipped up under her skirt from the canyon below. She wanted to believe that Logan could do what he claimed. She wanted to trust that God would honor her prayer of desperation.

Slowly, methodically, she released her grip on the rock. Her hands ached from their hold, but slowly she stretched her fingers until they were straight. She lifted her arm ever so slowly. She refused to look up, terrified that she would find the distance too far to make contact with Logan's hand. But then his hand clamped down on her wrist jarring her rigid body to her toes. Amelia had to force herself not to cry out.

"I've got you. Now just don't fight me and we'll be okay," Logan called down to her. "I'm going to pull you back up on the count of three. One. Two—"

Amelia's heart was in her throat. *If I die now there will never be any hope of reconciling myself to God.*

"Three!" Logan exclaimed and Amelia found herself being hoisted back up the rock wall. She heard her crepe de Chine skirt tear against the jagged edge and the loose dirt rolling off the ledge as Logan dragged her across it. In the time that it took to realize what had happened, Amelia lay atop the ground with Logan panting heavily at her side.

He jumped up quickly and pulled her away from the edge to more stable ground. Wrapping his arms around her, he held her in a trembling embrace that told her how afraid he'd been. He sighed against her ear and Amelia thought it all more wondrous than she could take in. She relished the warmth of his body against hers and the powerful hold of his arms. *He loves me,* she thought. If only she could stay in his arms forever.

Then, without warning, she started to giggle and then to laugh and Logan pulled away to look at her quite seriously. The thoughts flooding through her mind, however, would not let her even speak a word of explanation. It was almost as though the missing joy in her life had suddenly bubbled over inside.

"Amelia, are you all right?"

She nodded and continued to laugh so hard that tears came to her eyes.

"It's shock," he said authoritatively. "Come sit down."

Shaking, Amelia allowed him to lead her to a small boulder and sat willingly when he pushed her to do so. She was still laughing, however, at the very idea that she had asked God to give her a sign so clear that she could not miss the truth! What remained comical in her mind was that God could hardly have made it any clearer, and even Amelia, in her childish refusal to believe in His presence, was ready to admit her folly.

Logan sat down beside her and pulled her gently into his arms. She looked over and found his expression so fearful that it sent her into new peals of laughter.

"I'm sorry," she alternated between gasps and giggles. "It's just so, so—" her voice fell away in uncontrollable mirth.

"Amelia, honey, you've got to calm down," Logan said softly. Her hair had managed to come loose during her escapade up the mountain, and Logan methodically stroked it as if to calm her.

"It's just," she said, finally gaining control of her voice, "that I asked God to prove Himself to me. I asked Him for a sign that even I couldn't ignore and then He does just that, getting my full attention by dangling me over the ledge! Oh, Logan, don't you see how funny it is?"

Logan nodded and smiled. "I remember you asking Him for love, too."

This did the trick in sobering her completely. "Yes, I did." She looked deep into his eyes, unable to make out their brilliant green shading in the moonlight. "I'm glad you came."

"Me, too."

With their faces only inches apart, the kiss that followed seemed more than natural. Amelia felt Logan bury his warm fingers in her hair in order to slant her head just enough to give him free access to her mouth. She was stunned by the kiss at first, then a flaming warmth seemed to radiate out from where their lips touched. It flowed down through her body until Amelia wanted to shout aloud with joy.

"Amelia," Logan sighed her name as he pulled away from the kiss. "I love you, Amelia. Please tell me that you could love a barbarian."

She smiled. "I *do* love you, Logan Reed."

With this, he kissed her again, only this time less urgently and when he pulled away, Amelia could see that his eyes glistened. "I thought I'd lost you," he whispered.

"I couldn't see a reason to go on, but neither did I have the courage to put an end to my life," Amelia admitted.

"It doesn't take courage to kill yourself," Logan interjected. "That's the coward's way out."

"I was in such turmoil. I kept remembering the things my mother had taught me about God and the things you kept pushing in my face." At that she smiled and took hold of his hand. "Logan, you were right to keep after me. I've always known God existed, but I didn't want to admit it because if He existed in the power and glory people told me about, it also meant that He had the power to keep the bad things in my life from happening. But He didn't. He let Jeffery torture me as a child. He let my Mother die before I was ready to say good-bye to her and He left me to be forced into a marriage with a man I can't abide." She paused and searched Logan's face for condemnation. When she found only love reflected in his gaze, she continued.

"To believe in His existence meant I had to accept that He knew what was happening and that He stood by and let it happen. That seemed cruel and heartless to me. The God my mother had always told me of was merciful and loving. I couldn't accept that He would do such a thing or even allow someone else to do those things. Does that make any sense?"

"I think so," Logan replied. "But how about now? Those things haven't changed. And, there are still horrible tragedies in life. Tragedies that won't just go away overnight."

"That's true," Amelia said thoughtfully, "but I suppose I must simply accept that fact. I don't imagine life will always make sense, but what does make sense to me is that if there is a way to deal with the bad times in peace and confidence, then that's what I want. I've watched you all summer and your peace and assurance has driven me nearly insane."

He laughed at this and hugged her close. "Your uppity, stubborn 'I'll-do-it-myself' attitude has nearly driven me to drink, so I guess we're even." He ran his hand through the blond silk and smiled. "Oh, and I always wondered what you'd look like with your hair down and now I know."

"And what exactly do you know?" she asked impishly.

"That you are the most beautiful woman in the world," Logan replied. "What little of it, I've seen."

"There's no place else in the world as pretty as Estes, Logan, and no place I'd rather be."

"So what are we going to do, now?" he asked softly.

Amelia smiled and pulled back far enough to look into his face. "I'm ready to lay it all out before God, Logan. I'm ready to face life and march back down the mountain and do what I'm told to do." She bit at her lower lip and looked away before adding, "At least I think I am. It won't be easy to leave you."

"Leave me? Who said anything about you leaving me. I want you to marry me, Amelia."

She shook her head. "That, Logan, is impossible. There are things you don't know about which prevent my giving in to such a dream. And believe me, that is my dream. I would love to marry you and stay here in the mountains for the rest of my life. I know it deep down inside me, just as I know that I'm ready to accept Christ as my Savior." She paused feeling suddenly shy about her declarations. "But it is not possible for us to marry."

"With God," Logan said, reaching out to lift her face, "all things are possible. The Bible says so and I believe it with all of my heart, just as I believe you will one day be Mrs. Logan Reed."

Amelia felt tears come anew. She looked at him there in the moonlight and tried to commit to memory, every line and angle. She reached out and touched the mustache that she'd so often longed to touch and found it soft, yet coarse, against her fingers. Funny, but she'd not even noticed it when he'd kissed her.

She gazed into his eyes, seeing the longing and love reflected there for her—longing and love she held in her own heart for him. *How can I explain that I could never be his wife? How can I walk away from the only man I will ever love and marry another?*

As if sensing her thoughts, Logan took hold of her hand and kissed her fingers gently. "All things are possible with God," he repeated. "Not just some things, but all things."

"You don't understand, Logan. My father needs me to marry Jeffery. He owes him a great debt and Sir Chamberlain will brook no nonsense in collecting on the matter."

"Does he love you?" Logan asked quite seriously.

"No. I think that man incapable of love. But he does desire my land," she said smiling at the irony of it all. One man wanted her heart, another her land and she was stuck in the middle with her own longing and need and no one but God knew what that might mean to her.

"Do you love him?"

"Certainly not!" she declared with a look of horror.

"I love you, Amelia," He said simply. "I love you and I want to marry you, not for land or money or noble title, but because life without you would be unbearable. I think I fell in love with you the morning after our first all day ride. You tried so hard to keep from grimacing in pain as you got on that horse the next morning and I thought to myself, 'Here's a woman with real spirit.' Then I think I loved you even more when you went bustling around camp trying so hard to work at every job I gave you. I pushed you a bit too hard, but I got my reward. It put you in my arms."

"You asked me to choose between barbarians or twits," she murmured. "And you thought I chose Jeffery."

"No, I didn't."

"But you said—" she paused, cocking her head to one side as if to better understand him.

"I said that I could see you'd made your choice. I never said you chose Sir Twit. But I could see the argument you were having with yourself over feelings that you couldn't yet come to terms with. So I gave you over to him, hoping that the misery would drive you right back to me."

"I couldn't sleep that night for the things you made me feel," she admitted.

"Me either. So you see, I'm not ready to give up and say this can't be done. I'm quite willing to fight for you and pay off your father's debt if necessary."

"You can't. It's a great deal more money than either of us could hope to raise."

"How much?" he asked flatly, with a look of disbelief on his face.

"Seventy-thousand pounds."

"Done."

"Done?" she questioned. "Where in the world are you going to come up with seventy-thousand pounds?"

"Well, it probably won't be pounds, but American dollars will spend just the same."

She shook her head. "Don't joke about this."

"I'm not joking."

She could see by the serious expression on his face that indeed, he wasn't joking. "How are you going to come by seventy-thousand dollars or pounds?"

"I'll take it out of the bank."

"You mean rob it?" she asked in alarm.

Logan laughed until Amelia thought he would fall off the rock on which they were sitting. "No, silly. I'll withdraw that much from my account."

"You have that much money?"

"And a good deal more," he said soberly.

"But I thought—"

"You thought because I live here in Estes and lead guided tours into the park that I was too dirt poor to go anywhere else. Isn't that right?" She nodded, feeling quite guilty for her assessment. "Well, it isn't true. I've got more money than I'll ever need thanks to a little gold mine my father and I own. The truth is, I live this way because I love it. Estes is the only place in the world I ever came to that when I first laid eyes on it, I felt like I'd come home."

"Me, too," she whispered, barely able to speak. *Did God bring me here to bring me home to Him? To Logan?* It was more than she could take in all at once. *Is this how God is making Himself real in my life? To suddenly answer all my needs in one powerful stroke?*

Logan got to his knees and pulled her down with him. "First things first," he said, pulling her closer. "You said you were ready to accept Christ as your Savior, right?" Amelia nodded, forgetting everything else for a moment. "Then that is where we start our new life together," he replied and led her in a prayer of repentance.

sixteen

Snow blanketed the mountain tops while a light powdery dusting covered the valley below. They had left Estes days ago and Amelia felt an apprehension that grew into genuine fear. What if Logan couldn't convince her father to release her from the engagement to Sir Jeffery? What if Jeffery, himself, refused? With each step the horses took, with every descending clip of their hooves against the dirt and rocks, Amelia felt something inside her die.

She watched both men with anxious eyes, all the while praying fervently. Her father seemed mindless of her dilemma and Jeffery only appeared smug and self-satisfied with the circumstance. Logan promised that God would provide an answer and a way to see them through, but Amelia wasn't as steady in her faith as Logan and the possibility seemed completely out of reach.

Shortly before noon, Logan stopped the party to rest the horses and to Amelia's surprise he beckoned Sir Jeffery to follow him into the forest. Appearing quite annoyed with their barbaric guide, Jeffery did as he was bid, but not without a scowl of displeasure plastered across his aristocratic face. In a short while they returned to join the party and Jeffery seemed all smiles and satisfaction. Amelia was puzzled by this turn of events, but no more so than when Jeffery heralded her father and the two men began to have a feverish discussion. From time to time her father nodded and glanced in her direction, but no one summoned her or indicated a need for her presence and so Amelia remained with her horse, seeing to it that he was properly watered.

They remounted and made their way another hour or so, weaving back and forth across the St. Vrain River before emerging from the canyon to face some six miles of flat prairie land. Longmont would be at the end of that prairie ground and Amelia felt her hope giving way. Longmont represented the place where they were to take the stage to Denver and forever leave Estes, and Logan, behind them. She shuddered, fought back tears and prayed for strength to endure whatever God decided. And all the while she felt her heart nearly breaking with desire to turn around and run back to the safety of Estes.

How could she leave?

She glanced over her shoulder to the mountains. They seemed gray in the harsher light, and the chill in the air left little doubt that winter would soon be a serious business in the area. She gripped the reins tighter and ignored the single tear which slid down her cheek.

How could she leave Logan?

She watched him lead the way across the dried-out prairie and tried to imagine sitting in her damp, drafty English manor house without him. Months ago, she wouldn't have given a single shilling to extend her trip to America by even a day, and now she knew she'd gladly trade the rest of her life to be able to marry Logan and share even a few days as his wife.

"I say," the earl called out to his companions, "this place seems worse for the passing of time."

"Indeed," Lord Gambett replied, gazing about. "Not at all pleasant. It was hot and unbearable when we departed and now we find it dusty and devoid of life."

Amelia smiled at this. Months ago, she would have agreed with Lord Gambett, but now, with the training Logan had given her, Amelia observed life everywhere. Insects, animals, autumn vegetation. It was all there, it was just a matter of where you looked.

"Whoa," she heard Logan call to the party. She glanced forward to find that everyone had halted their horses on the edge of town. "I believe you all know your way from here," Logan said sternly. "Tie up your mounts in front of the hotel and take your personal belongings with you. I'll see to the horses and gear and meet you to settle up in about half an hour. I'll also bring your trunks at that time."

Everyone nodded and urged their horses forward to the hotel. Amelia saw her father and Mattersley press forward with Penelope and Margaret in tow, but she couldn't bring herself to join them. She stared, instead, at Logan astride his horse. Logan, whose face was tanned and sported a new two-day growth of beard. Logan, whose jeans accented his well-muscled legs and whose indigo-dyed, cambric shirt hugged him in way Amelia longed to imitate. He pulled off his hat, wiped his brow and finally noticed that she was watching him. With a grin, he replaced the hat and nudged his horse in her direction.

"You having trouble following directions again, Lady Amhurst?"

She felt a lump in her throat that threatened to strangle her. "No," she barely croaked out.

His mustache twitched as he broke into a broad smile. "Faith, Amelia. Have faith."

"It's stronger when I'm with you," she replied.

"Don't put your faith in me. Remember, your strength comes from God and He will help you."

She nodded. "Okay, Logan. My faith is in God." She spoke the words aloud hoping it would help her to feel more confident. "But how are we going to—"

"Don't worry about anything. Now join up with your family and I'll see you in half an hour." He winked at her before leading his horse off in the direction of the livery.

"Don't worry—have faith," she murmured and urged her mount forward. "Easier said than done."

❧

Half an hour later, Amelia was just as nervous as when she'd left Logan. Her father seemed preoccupied with some matter, while Sir Jeffery was suddenly paying far more attention to Penelope and Margaret than he'd done throughout the entire trip. When she could stand it no longer, Amelia went to the earl and demanded to know what was going on.

"Amelia, Sir Jeffery has agreed to release you from your engagement."

Her mouth dropped. Recovering her composure she asked, "He did? But what of the money?" At this Mattersley took several steps away from the earl and pretended to be preoccupied by studying the ceiling.

Her father shrugged. "He dismissed the debt as well. I have no idea what you said to him, Amelia, but there it is."

"But I don't understand."

"It would seem that you have won this round. I. . .well. . . perhaps I was overly influenced to marry you off because of the debt." He looked at her intently. "I never meant any harm by it, Amelia. I thought you could be happy in time. I suppose now you are free to remain unmarried."

"But what of the inheritance and your concerns for the family coffers?" she asked warily.

Weariness seemed to mar his brow. "You gave your word that you'd not see us suffer and I've always known you to be a woman of truth. Having you stay on with me as your sisters marry and leave, will no doubt be a comfort in my old age."

How strange, Amelia thought wondering how she might broach the subject of Logan's proposal and her own desire to remain in America. How could she explain the change in her heart when she'd been the one to protest leaving England in the first place?

"Ah, good, you're all here," Logan said, striding into the room as though he were about to lead them all in a lecture symposium.

Lord Amhurst looked up with Mattersley doing likewise, but Penelope and Margaret remained in animated conversation with Sir Jeffery. Lord and Lady Gambett stared up wearily from their chairs, while Henrietta and Josephine looked as though they might start whining at any given moment. Amelia dared to catch Logan's gaze and when he smiled warmly at her it melted away some of the fear she felt.

"Your trunks are outside," he announced, "and the stage is due in two hours. I'd suggest you take one of your breaks for tea and cakes before heading to Denver. There isn't much in between here and there, and you'll be mighty sorry if you don't."

"I believe this will square our account," Lord Gambett said, extending an envelope.

Logan looked the contents over and nodded. "This is mighty generous of you, Gambett." The man seemed notably embarrassed and merely nodded before muttering something about seeing to the trunks.

"And this should account for us," Lord Amhurst announced, providing a similar envelope.

Logan tucked the envelope into his pocket without even looking. "If you have a moment, I'd like to speak with you privately, Lord Amhurst."

"I dare say, time is short, speak your mind Reed. We haven't even secured our tickets for the stage."

"They're reserved in your name, I assure you. Five tickets for Denver."

"Five? You mean six, don't you? Or did you reserve Sir Jeffery's separately?"

"No, I meant five." Logan looked at Amelia and held out

his hand to her.

Amelia hesitated only a second before joining Logan. Even Penelope and Margaret gasped at the sight of their sister holding hands with their American guide. Mattersley was the only one to offer even the slightest look of approval and that came in the form of a tight-lipped smile.

"I've asked Amelia to marry me, and she said yes. Now, I'm asking for your blessing, Lord Amhurst."

"Why I've never heard of such rubbish!" the earl exclaimed. "Amelia, what nonsense is this man speaking?"

"It isn't nonsense, Father." Amelia noted that her sisters had gathered closer, while Lady Gambett, seeing a major confrontation in the making, ushered her girls into the dining room. Jeffery stood by looking rather bored and indifferent. She smiled up at Logan and tried to calm her nerves. "It's all true. I would very much like to marry Logan Reed and since Sir Jeffery has kindly released me from our betrothal, I am hoping to have your blessing."

"Never! You are the daughter of an earl. You've been presented at court and have the potential to marry. . .well. . .to certainly marry better than an American!"

"But I love an American," Amelia protested. "I can do no better than to marry for love."

"I forbid it!"

"Father, I'm nearly twenty-one," Amelia reminded him. "I can marry without your consent, but I'd much rather have it."

"You marry this man and I'll cut off all inheritance and funding from you. You'll never be welcomed to set foot on my property again."

"Isn't that what Grandfather Amhurst told you when you decided to marry Mother?" Penelope and Margaret both gasped in unison and fanned themselves furiously as though they might faint.

The earl reddened at the collar and looked quite uncomfortable. "That was a different circumstance."

"Not so very different to my way of thinking." Amelia dropped her hold on Logan and gently touched her father's arm. "Father, don't you want me to know true love as you and Mother did?"

"And you love this man enough to lose your fortune?"

"She doesn't need a fortune," Logan interjected. "I have enough for the both of us." This drew everyone's attention. "Look, there doesn't need to be any pretense between any of us." Logan drew out two envelopes and handed them to the earl. "I won't take your money for the trip and you can give this back to Lord Gambett, as well. Also," he said, reaching in for yet another envelope, "this is yours Chamberlain. You will find one hundred-thousand dollars awaiting you at the bank in Denver."

"One-hundred thousand?" Amelia questioned.

Logan smiled. "I had to make it worth his trouble." Jeffery said nothing, but tucked the envelope into his pocket. Lord Amhurst stood staring at his own envelopes while Logan continued. "As I said, Amelia doesn't need the Donneswick fortune. She'll be well-cared for by me and she won't want for anything, unless of course, it's your blessing."

The earl looked positively torn and Amelia instantly felt sorry for her father. "I love him, Father," she said, tears glistening in her eyes. "You wanted me to marry before my twenty-first birthday and I'm finally agreeing to that."

"Yes, but—" he looked at her and suddenly all the harshness of the last year seemed to fade from his expression. He looked from Amelia to Logan, and seemed to consider the idea as if for the first time. "I say, you truly wish to be married to him and live here, in America?"

"I truly do." She leaned over and kissed her father on the cheek, whispering in his ear, "Logan makes me happy, Papa.

Please say yes."

He smiled and touched Amelia's cheek. "You will come for visits, won't you?

"Of course we will," she replied. "So long as we're both welcomed."

He sighed. "Then you have my blessing, although I offer it up with some misgivings."

"Oh, thank you, Father. Thank you!" Amelia gave him an uncharacteristic public embrace before throwing herself into Logan's arms.

Logan hugged her tightly and happily obliged her when Amelia lifted her lips to his for a kiss.

"Ah, I say," the earl interrupted the passionate display, "but I don't suppose we could find a man of the cloth in this town, what?"

Logan broke the kiss and nodded. "Parson's waiting for us as we speak. I didn't figure you'd much want to leave her here without seeing her properly wed."

The earl very ceremoniously took out a pocket watch and popped open the cover. "Then I say we'd best be going about it. I have a stage to catch shortly, as you know."

epilogue

"I thought you said May around here would signal spring," Amelia said, rising slowly with a hand on her slightly swollen abdomen. She looked out the cabin window for the tenth time that morning and for the tenth time found nothing but snow to stare back at her.

"Hey," Logan said, coming up from behind her, "we didn't make such bad use of the winter." He wrapped his arms around her and felt the baby's hefty kick. "See, our son agrees."

"What he agrees with," Amelia said in her very formal English accent, "is that if his mother doesn't get out of this cabin soon, she's going to be stark raving mad."

"We could read together," Logan suggested. "We could get all cozied up under the covers for warmth, maybe throw in some heated rocks from the fireplace to keep our feet all toasty—" His words trailed off as he nuzzled her neck.

"I believe we've read every book in the cabin, at least twice," she said, enjoying his closeness.

"We could play a game of cards. We could get all cozied up—"

"I know. I know," she interrupted. "Under the covers for warmth and throw in some heated rocks, but honestly Logan I'm going to throw one of those rocks through the window if we can't do something other than sit here and count snowflakes."

"Maybe, just maybe, if you can bear to be parted from me for a spell, I'll ride down to Mary's and see if she can come up here for a bit. Maybe you ladies could share quilting secrets."

"But I want to get out! I want to walk around and see something other than four walls and frosted windows. I may be with child, but that certainly doesn't mean I'm without feet on which to walk. Please, Logan."

Logan sighed and laid his chin atop her head. "If you promise to dress very warmly and to wear your highest boots, and do everything I say, then I suppose I could be persuaded to—"

"Oh, Logan, truly?" Amelia whirled around causing Logan's head to snap back from the absence of support. "When can we go? Can we go now?"

Logan laughed, rubbed his chin and gave Amelia a look that said it all. She liked the way he was looking at her. It was a look that suggested that she alone was responsible for his happiness and if they remained snowed in the cabin for another six months, he'd still smile in just exactly the same way. He touched her cheek with his calloused fingers and smiled. "Good things take time, Lady Amhurst."

"Mrs. Reed," she corrected. "I'm happily no longer a lady of noble standing."

He grinned roguishly. "Oh, you're a lady, all right. But you're my lady now."

She smiled and felt a surge of joy bubble up inside her. "God sure had a way of getting my attention," she said, putting her hand over his.

"The stubborn, impatient ones are always the hardest," he whispered before lowering his mouth to hers.

Amelia wrapped her arms around Logan's neck and returned his kiss with great enthusiasm. She'd found the happiness that she'd never thought possible, and come September, she was going to have a baby. Logan's baby—and she was Logan's lady, and somehow that made the long winter seem not quite so unbearable.

A Letter To Our Readers

Dear Reader:

In order that we might better contribute to your reading enjoyment, we would appreciate your taking a few minutes to respond to the following questions. When completed, please return to the following:

Rebecca Germany, Managing Editor
Heartsong Presents
P.O. Box 719
Uhrichsville, Ohio 44683

1. Did you enjoy reading *Logan's Lady?*
   ❑ Very much. I would like to see more books by this author!
   ❑ Moderately
   I would have enjoyed it more if _____
   _____

2. Are you a member of **Heartsong Presents**? ❑Yes ❑No
   If no, where did you purchase this book? _____
   _____

3. What influenced your decision to purchase this book? (Check those that apply.)

   ❑ Cover   ❑ Back cover copy
   ❑ Title   ❑ Friends
   ❑ Publicity   ❑ Other_____

4. How would you rate, on a scale from 1 (poor) to 5 (superior), the cover design? _____

5. On a scale from 1 (poor) to 10 (superior), please rate the following elements.

___Heroine   ___Plot

___Hero   ___Inspirational theme

___Setting   ___Secondary characters

6. What settings would you like to see covered in **Heartsong Presents** books?_____

_____

_____

7. What are some inspirational themes you would like to see treated in future books?_____

_____

_____

8. Would you be interested in reading other **Heartsong Presents** titles?   ❏ Yes   ❏ No

9. Please check your age range:
   ❏ Under 18   ❏ 18-24   ❏ 25-34
   ❏ 35-45   ❏ 46-55   ❏ Over 55

10. How many hours per week do you read? _____

Name _____

Occupation_____

Address_____

City_____ State_____ Zip_____

APPLES FOR A TEACHER

LESSON PLANS FOR LIFE

COLLEEN L. REECE
ANITA CORRINE DONIHUE

Apples for A Teacher is a bushel of short stories, poems, and prayers meant to delight and encourage teachers from any classroom. Offering a refreshing perspective on this profession, these apples are little ways that all say "Thank you for being my teacher." A perfect gift book that will be treasured by special teachers everywhere! 64 pages, Hardbound, 5" x 6 ½"

Hearts♥ng

HEARTSONG PRESENTS TITLES AVAILABLE NOW:

__HP 40 PERFECT LOVE, *Janelle Jamison*
__HP 63 THE WILLING HEART, *Janelle Jamison*
__HP 64 CROWS'-NESTS AND MIRRORS, *Colleen L. Reece*
__HP103 LOVE'S SHINING HOPE, *JoAnn A. Grote*
__HP104 HAVEN OF PEACE, *Carol Mason Parker*
__HP111 A KINGDOM DIVIDED, *Tracie J. Peterson*
__HP112 CAPTIVES OF THE CANYON, *Colleen L. Reece*
__HP115 SISTERS IN THE SUN, *Shirley Rhode*
__HP124 HIS NAME ON HER HEART, *Mary LaPietra*
__HP127 FOREVER YOURS, *Tracie J. Peterson*
__HP128 MISPLACED ANGEL, *VeraLee Wiggins*
__HP131 LOVE IN THE PRAIRIE WILDS, *Robin Chandler*
__HP132 LOST CREEK MISSION, *Cheryl Tenbrook*
__HP135 SIGN OF THE SPIRIT, *Kay Cornelius*
__HP140 ANGEL'S CAUSE, *Tracie J. Peterson*
__HP143 MORNING MOUNTAIN, *Peggy Darty*

__HP144 FLOWER OF THE WEST, *Colleen L. Reece*
__HP147 DREWRY'S BLUFF, *Cara McCormack*
__HP148 DREAMS OF THE PIONEERS, *Linda Herring*
__HP155 TULSA TEMPEST, *Norma Jean Lutz*
__HP163 DREAMS OF GLORY, *Linda Herring*
__HP164 ALAS MY LOVE, *Tracie J. Peterson*
__HP167 PRISCILLA HIRES A HUSBAND, *Loree Lough*
__HP168 LOVE SHALL COME AGAIN, *Birdie L. Etchison*
__HP171 TULSA TURNING, *Norma Jean Lutz*
__HP172 A WHISPER OF SAGE, *Esther Loewen Vogt*
__HP175 JAMES'S JOY, *Cara McCormack*
__HP176 WHERE THERE IS HOPE, *Carolyn R. Scheidies*
__HP179 HER FATHER'S LOVE, *Nancy Lavo*
__HP180 FRIEND OF A FRIEND, *Jill Richardson*
__HP183 A NEW LOVE, *VeraLee Wiggins*
__HP184 THE HOPE THAT SINGS, *JoAnn A. Grote*

(If ordering from this page, please remember to include it with the order form.)

······· Presents ·······

Great Inspirational Romance at a Great Price!

Heartsong Presents books are inspirational romances in contemporary and historical settings, designed to give you an enjoyable, spirit-lifting reading experience. You can choose wonderfully written titles from some of today's best authors like Peggy Darty, Sally Laity, Tracie J. Peterson, Colleen L. Reece, Lauraine Snelling, and many others.

When ordering quantities less than twelve, above titles are $2.95 each.
Not all titles may be available at time of order.

SEND TO: Heartsong Presents Reader's Service
P.O. Box 719, Uhrichsville, Ohio 44683

Please send me the items checked above. I am enclosing $_____
(please add $1.00 to cover postage per order. OH add 6.25% tax. NJ add 6%). Send check or money order, no cash or C.O.D.s, please.
To place a credit card order, call 1-800-847-8270.

NAME _____

ADDRESS _____

CITY/STATE_____ ZIP _____

HPS 9-97

Heartsong Presents
Love Stories Are Rated G!

That's for godly, gratifying, and of course, great! If you love a thrilling love story, but don't appreciate the sordidness of some popular paperback romances, **Heartsong Presents** is for you. In fact, **Heartsong Presents** is the *only inspirational romance book club*, the only one featuring love stories where Christian faith is the primary ingredient in a marriage relationship.

Sign up today to receive your first set of four, never before published Christian romances. Send no money now; you will receive a bill with the first shipment. You may cancel at any time without obligation, and if you aren't completely satisfied with any selection, you may return the books for an immediate refund!

Imagine. . .four new romances every four weeks—two historical, two contemporary—with men and women like you who long to meet the one God has chosen as the love of their lives. . .all for the low price of $9.97 postpaid.

To join, simply complete the coupon below and mail to the address provided. **Heartsong Presents** romances are rated G for another reason: They'll arrive *Godspeed!*